Fumiko,
    This one is like the
first "Father's Day"...
on steroids!
        Enjoy!
        Gary Kyuaji
        June 22. 2021

FATHER'S DAY

Part II - The Secret of La Sangre

GARY KYRIAZI

outskirts
press

To my Family and Friends.
Thank you for 70 wonderful years.

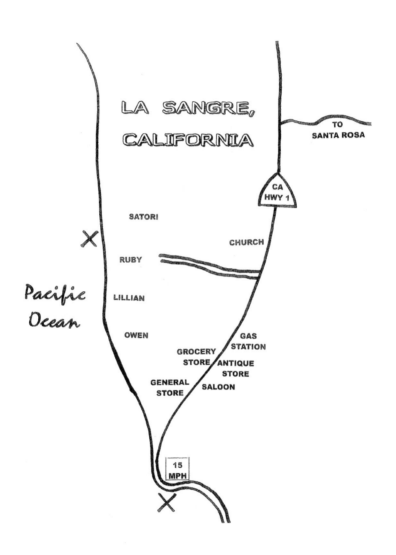

LA SANGRE, CALIFORNIA

SATURDAY, JUNE 15, 1985
FATHER'S DAY EVE
9 PM

ONE

Sal Satori fell asleep on his recliner just as the mantle clock chimed nine and "Hill Street Blues" began. He was exhausted. He had toiled, in vain, on tomorrow's sermon for Father's Day, a holiday that everyone in La Sangre, himself especially, would like to forget about after what happened last year.

The melodic theme song of "Hill Street Blues" kept on playing, well past the opening credits. Sal wondered why it kept playing over and over, and the story hadn't begun. He made himself wake up.

The TV was off, and his three-month-old son Freeman was no longer in the playpen near him. Connie must have turned the TV off and taken Freeman upstairs to bed. What time was it?

The mantle clock still read nine. Did it stop? In response the clock began to chime. Sal counted nine rings. It was the second time it had chimed nine. Had he actually slept for twelve hours? It wasn't daylight out, but instead the orange glare of the sunset. A sunset at 9 PM? Too late.

"Connie?" he called out.

No answer.

She often took the baby outside to the deck, so he got up and opened the front door. Connie wasn't there. He walked to the end of the deck before realizing that he was nude. He never sat around the house or slept nude, he always had his boxers on, sometimes a tee shirt, upstairs anyway. Downstairs he'd wear jeans and usually a polo shirt in case someone from town knocked, in need of spiritual guidance.

But now he was standing where the entire town of La Sangre, California, could see him. Their Pastor, standing naked on the deck of his house, against a surreal angry-orange sunset that promised no change, no mellowing. This ungodly sunset, almost an hour late this time of the year, was here to stay.

The deck stairs went down to the grassy bluff, where the well-worn path led 150 feet straight to the cliff with its 70-foot drop to the ocean. A left fork in the path led to the other homes, and a right fork led to where the 50-foot-high rock marked the northern boundary of La Sangre. ("Peter The Rock," the townspeople called it.) California State Route 1 had to curve around the rock as it ventured north along the treacherous Northern California coast. Sal had long wanted to place a cross on the top of the rock, like the cross atop Mount Davidson, the highest point in San Francisco. But the California Coastal Commission wouldn't let him, no surprise there.

But now in his dream, Sal looked up at the rock to imagine a white cross hovering over and protecting La Sangre. How beautiful that would be, what a fine witness it would make. It would attract people, they'd stop in town, use the businesses, maybe visit the church with its stained-glass windows, and later maybe even attend Sunday service if they lived in the nearby coastal towns of Jenner, Bodega Bay, or Point Reyes Station.

But wait, there already *was* a cross up on the rock. When did that happen? It was white, it was clean.

Sal gasped.

It was upside down.

Connie listened to Sal's mournful sleep from the kitchen. She had checked to make sure it wasn't scaring Freeman, who was in his crib in the middle of the living room. But he was having fun, wiggling and joyfully grasping at the toy mobile suspended above him. Normally Sal had his recurring nightmare at 2 AM, this was a first, at 9 PM.

"Freeman, I think it's time for your supper," she said loudly, not caring if she woke Sal. She went over to the crib, picked him up, and sat down on her favorite chair, not a recliner but comfortable. Once she adjusted her blouse and bra and he started in, she began to talk to him.

"Freeman, I'm really getting tired of this. Oh no, sweetie, not you. You're all I've got. I haven't seen your brother—half-brother—Corey in almost a year, and he hasn't even met you. I guess he still hates me, and I can't blame him. You don't hate me, do you Freeman?" He bit down hard. "Ouch! Very funny!" She grinned at her three-month-old son. Freeman was now the only thing in her life that could bring a smile to her still-youthful 35-year-old face.

"You know what we're going to do? We're going to spend the rest of our lives together, just you and me. Yes, we're going to leave your father because sweetie, I'm tired of this crap." She chuckled. "I'm tired of not being able to say 'crap' because I'm a 'Pastor's Wife.' Tired of my childhood as 'Connie Cooty,' tired of being loved one time and getting pregnant at 17, being carted off to Fresno so I could discretely have Corey because 'what would the neighbors and the people at church and the kids at school think?' I'm tired of being married to a man who doesn't love me...not for lack of trying, I'll give him that. And I'm tired of performing as a pastor's wife, playing the organ during the services, pretending to listen attentively to a sermon he already rehearsed to me, listening patiently to the congregation's various problems, and offering them unanswered prayers."

Not interrupting his meal, Freeman looked up at his mother with his father's brown eyes.

"All right son, maybe their prayers are answered, I don't know. But my prayers sure aren't, like for my other son, your older brother. Am I ever going to see him again? Is he ever going to call me, or at least write?"

Sal moaned in the recliner. Freeman bit down again.

"Ouch! Don't worry sweetie, it's just your father having his nightmare."

Connie had stopped waking Sal from his nightmares after the first three months of it. Let him deal with it, it didn't bother her or Freeman.

Sal shut his eyes against the upside-down cross, but he could still see it through his eyelids. So he turned to the ocean, the steady and constant ocean, the reliable sight and sound of God.

But the ocean was silent. No sound at all from the waves that charged in and crashed against the rocks at the bottom of the cliff. This silence was even louder than the ocean itself could ever be. So it was wrong...but somehow, maybe right. Right/wrong. One or the other, it didn't matter. He knew that in some way he belonged here, in this ambivalent world, where right and wrong were irrelevant.

Needing to get closer to the ocean, however

menacingly silent, he went down the deck steps to the bluff, relishing the fresh green grass and soft dirt between his toes and around his feet. Yes, this part was right. Nice.

"Nice, isn't it Sal?" said a familiar, confident, feminine voice.

He looked over to the right, where Jessie stood 25 yards away, the grass just past her ankles. She too was nude, her lithe body reminding him of how nice it was, their one tryst exactly a year ago, a moment of exhilarating madness that was still within his accessible memory, however hard he had tried to flush it out. He'd worn himself out trying to exorcise that memory. But that body, a natural woman's body, a body that she could love and take her own pleasure with, with no need to shape it into what a man's idea of what a woman's body was. She had given it freely to him. He could still feel how soft and warm it was against him, the gentle strength she gave him, if for just that one hour, an hour he apparently will spend the rest of his life taking pleasure in. Loving it. And hating it. Loving/hating it. No, loving it.

"Jessie?" he softly called, and became aroused.

"That's right, Sal," she smiled with approval.

He nodded, then shook his head. This was wrong. This was right. Right/wrong, wrong/ right. He was sick and tired of bouncing back and forth within his black and white existence.

Gray was necessary, gray was a part of life; at least he tried to convince himself of that.

"The devil loves gray, Sal," said another familiar voice, a man's voice. "It can be a dangerous playground."

Sal turned from Jessie and looked straight ahead, at the man standing with his back to the edge of the cliff, facing him.

"Jay?"

Jay Carpenter, six-foot-five, 225 pounds with his blazing long red beard, was wearing the same red plaid jacket, jeans and hiking boots of last year, and accompanied by the same Irish Setter, Barnabas.

"Jay? Where have you been?"

"Here, there, busy. But I've had help. Look," Jay pointed to Sal's left. Sal turned.

Nicholas Salvatore Satori was standing the same distance away from Sal as Jessie was.

"Dad?"

"Hello Son."

"Can I...come to you?"

Nick shook his head. "No Sal, stay there."

"All right, but Dad, tell me why...."

"Why did your Mom and I die so young?"

Sal nodded, tears suddenly flowing.

"It was God's will, Sal."

"God's will, but it doesn't make any sense to me!"

"I know that. I know it's been hard for you.

But your Mom and I were hoping that the nice estate we left you would make life easier for you. At least you wouldn't have to struggle financially, if you invested it wisely. But we didn't expect you to spend it all on..." Nick Satori waved his hand around La Sangre. "You spent all the money we left you here, buying the businesses, buying at least half of the homes. I'm sure the real estate investment is good, son, but you're...."

"Stuck. Really stuck Dad."

"Do you know *why* you did it? Were you trying to create your own heaven?"

"Dad, I was..." Sal choked on his tears. "I was...trying to get God to like me. The loving part was easy, but I just wanted Him to *like* me! The way you liked me. Remember how you cheered for me in the ring as a kid; you knew I was good, you never missed a bout!"

"I loved watching you. Your mother couldn't watch, that's why she didn't go."

"I know, that was okay." Sal sniffed and wiped his cheeks with his wrist, the tears slowed.

"Sal, I wish I could have talked you out of going into the ministry. I told you it was a thankless job, no tangible returns, but you were determined."

"There were souls to save, Dad. And I failed. I failed Connie, Corey, La Sangre, now I have another son, and I'm afraid I'll fail him too."

"Give yourself a break son. Take it easy."

"He's right, Sal," Jessie said from behind him. "Take it easy. Remember what I told you that night: we're not sinners because we sin, we sin because we're sinners."

He turned back around to her. She was still standing there, not especially waiting, she was just there, ready when he was. "Yes, I'm here Sal," she confirmed. But fifty feet above her was the upside-down cross. This isn't right. He knew it. He knew it in his gut. This was definitely wrong. Not right/wrong, not gray, just wrong.

Sal instinctively turned to his right to look at his house, his home. Connie was inside, with Freeman. Corey was gone, he never wrote or called.

"I'm with Corey," Jay said from behind Sal.

Sal turned back to Jay. "Is he all right?" But Jay didn't answer.

"Dad," Sal turned to his left, "do you know? He's your grandson."

His father didn't answer either, but pointed to Sal's left. "Look."

Between Sal and the house, a ten-foot wide section of ground sunk quickly and silently, extending north to the rock and south along the California coastline. Sal took a few tentative steps toward it and looked into blackness. There was no bottom, and it was too wide for him to jump across. California's San Andreas Fault Line. So, it was time. He could never go home again. Some geologists and self-proclaimed prophets were saying this year, 1985, would be the Big One. California would fall into the ocean. He turned back to his father.

"So, this is it?" Sal asked him.

"If you don't have your gloves on, Son." Another ten-foot-wide fissure sunk between Sal and his father, intersecting the first one and extending from the cliff, across Highway 1, and into the coastal hills.

"Jay?" Sal turned to him. The ground was still solid between them.

"Yes Sal?"

"Don't move."

"I won't."

Sal began walking towards him, but a third fissure sunk, parallel to the cliff, separating him from Jay, leaving solid ground only to his right, leading to Jessie, and the upside-down cross above her.

"You mean," Sal exclaimed to Jay, "*she's* the only way I can go? Are you going to leave me here like this, with just her haunting my brain, tearing me up, ruining my marriage? Thanks a lot man."

Jay smiled lightly and nodded. "I'll never let you down, Sal, you know that. But you've got to man up. Now, run and jump over it, to me."

"It's...it's too *wide*!"

"Run and jump Sal!" his father encouraged

him. "Not to me, to Jay."

To his right, Jessie laughed. "Run and jump Sal!" she mimicked Jay's tone. "But Sal, you don't have to run and jump. It's solid ground over to me. Solid ground, very real. Real and right."

"Wrong," Sal responded weakly.

"Right, wrong, what's the difference?" Jessie kept laughing. "You said so yourself. Life is gray, relax and enjoy it."

Sal turned to his left, back towards his Dad, but he was gone, the fissure still there. He looked over at Jay, who was waiting.

"Hey, I'm getting tired of this! Haven't I done enough penance for the past year?" he screamed at Jay. "How much more am I going to have to pay? Pray and pay, that's all I've done!"

"It's already paid for, Sal." Jay held his arms up. "Come on man, just run and jump!"

Sal, ever pragmatic, even in his dream state, considered his options. He couldn't go home, couldn't go to his father, or even to Jay. The fissures were too wide. There was only one way he could go.

Sal turned to the right and walked towards Jessie.

"Sal," she smiled warmly, waiting.

"Jessie!"

TWO

Sal's scream didn't bother Freeman at all, who continued with his meal. Connie just looked at Sal, in his recliner, wide-eyed, his polo shirt sweat-stained. She suddenly knew this was the last time.

"No Sal, my name is Connie, not Jessie, *Connie*. And this is your son, Freeman...who I think just finished his supper."

"Oh God Connie," Sal lay his head back. "I'm sorry."

"Again?" Connie removed Freeman from her bosom and put him back in the crib. She buttoned her top. "It doesn't matter." She was going to go back in the kitchen to finish whatever she was doing, but instead sat down. This was it. "Oh, it used to matter," she sighed. "Like that time when we had wild sex, like we never had before. That was exactly a year ago. The night before Father's Day, just like now. Oh, you were beautiful, Sal, a real Italian stallion as you and I often kid, and then you said her name."

"Connie please, it was just that one time."

"One time awake, you mean. I've had to listen to her name in your nightmares since then." She smiled sardonically. "Oh, but during all that wonderful, wild sex we've had since then, this past year, even if you didn't mention her name you were still thinking of her, weren't you? I was just a tool, your ever-dutiful spouse. The Pastor's Wife."

"But Connie, I thought you...."

"Oh yes, I enjoyed it Sal. I loved it. But just the same it wasn't me you were making love to."

"You know how much I'm trying, I've been talking to Ralph..."

"Yes, Dr. Ralph Owen, the psychiatrist, who owns the home that Jessie was renting last year. Is that just another way of keeping her alive? Being in that house whenever you talk to him? Do you look at where it happened, in the bedroom maybe?"

It was a one-two-three punch, and Sal was on the mat, hearing the final count through a fog. ("One! Two! Three! Four! Five....")

Connie leaned back in her chair. "You know Sal, most women just have to worry about the postpartum stuff, the extra pounds, the 'Does my husband still find me attractive?' thing. But I have to deal with a dead woman."

"Connie, you can't...forgive me?"

She looked at his face. That still very handsome face, light olive skin and black hair, the newly graying sideburns further enhancing him. "No Sal. I think we're past forgiveness and just down to the facts now."

"The facts," Sal repeated dubiously.

"Yes, like I'm going back to Bakersfield."

"Move back in with your parents?"

She frowned. "Doesn't that sound awful? Not the moving back in with my folks part, but just 'Going back to Bakersfield?' I mean, people *leave* Bakersfield, they don't go *back* there." She sighed. "No, I don't know exactly what or how I'm doing it, but I'm leaving you. Don't worry, we'll get a lawyer, you'll always be able to see your son. I don't know how it's done, but everyone else does it. I don't see why a pastor and his wife can't do it."

"Connie..." Sal turned to look at her, but she avoided his eyes.

"Do you want me to fix you a sandwich? A glass of milk? It's almost a full moon tonight, go out to the cliff and look at it. Watch the ocean. Work on your Father's Day sermon. Pray. Whatever. Freeman and I are going upstairs to bed. You can sleep in our marriage bed, this last time. But no sex, unless it's me you're making love to."

The phone rang.

"Oh, that's probably Grace. We made a phone date for nine. Go on, take your walk."

It wasn't until Sal put on his Nikes, grabbed his jacket and stepped out the front door onto the deck that he could fully absorb what Connie had just told him. By the time he reached the steps, he not only absorbed it, it was neatly filed. It took him a whole six seconds to absorb and file something that he knew was coming over the last year. Exactly a year, like Connie said. The night before Father's Day. Now, for the first time in his 13 years of pastoring the La Sangre Christian Church, he didn't sanction or even mention a Father's Day picnic. The congregation knew better than to bring it up after what had happened last year.

But if he could so easily process and file away the fact that his wife was leaving him and taking his boy, why couldn't he do the same with Jessie, who's dead and gone?

Indeed Sal. Why not?

Well because, that night, that special magical night, for just one hour, he had had the greatest sex he'd ever known, with Jessie, at the house she rented from the Owens. "Remember our wild fucking under the table, Sal, the next time you say the blessing before a meal," Jessie had told him when she triumphantly showed him the door. He went home and showered, went to the church to pray for forgiveness; Connie found him there, and then they went home where they had the greatest sex they'd ever had in their 17 years of marriage. If only he hadn't shouted out "JESSIE!" in the middle of his ecstasy.

Connie had forgiven him then, as easily as she had forgiven him when he confessed his adultery to her just two hours earlier that same night. Just like he had forgiven her when she confessed that all during their marriage she thought she was in love with Peter Freeman, Corey's father, and that's why she could never fully give herself to Sal.

Pray, forgive, perform as Pastor-and-Wife, smile, listen to the trials and tribulations of the people of La Sangre, run the businesses on Highway 1, collect the rents, handle the maintenance, pray, forgive...it was a carousel. A Christian Carousel, with no joy.

Sal himself had spent the last year trying to change; really, sincerely, trying to become more human, more...whatever he was to become "more" of. ("Relax and enjoy life, son," his father had advised him in the dream.) When he'd told Dr. Owen about the dream during one of their talks, particularly what his father said, Dr. Owen agreed, "That's not bad advice."

But Sal couldn't do it. The tide of his emotions, his spirit, ran either low or high, from choking repression to wild abandon. Would he ever settle in the middle? *Could* he ever settle in the middle, live in it, peacefully? Could he ever *relax*?

Sal was so deep in his thoughts that he hadn't noticed Dr. Ralph Owen standing about 100 feet ahead of him at the cliff, alone, looking at the ocean. "I'm enjoying it more and more," Ralph had recently told Sal, "looking at the ocean, listening. Who knows, maybe I'm praying." Sal had closed his eyes and nodded in doubtful indulgence, but looking at Ralph now, he wasn't so sure. *Was* Ralph actually praying? Sal stopped, respecting Ralph's solitude, realizing that he saw Ralph clearly in the moonlight because, unusually, there was no fog. But the seagulls hadn't gone to sleep, they were squawking angrily. Just like last year, no fog and mad seagulls on the night before Father's Day.

Two figures suddenly approached Ralph from the dirt road leading to Highway 1: a tall woman with long hair, and a monster of a man who dominated even Dr. Owen. Neither of them noticed Sal's presence, focused as they were on Ralph. Sal heard their voices, muffled by the ocean, but couldn't hear what they were saying to Ralph until the gigantic man screamed "YOU DON'T DO THAT TO CHILDREN!"

Sal hesitated.

"YOU DON'T DO THAT TO CHILDREN!" The gargantuan stepped toward Ralph in obvious threat.

Alerted, Sal walked toward the threesome with purpose, remembering what Jay Carpenter had told him in his recurring nightmare...which wasn't a nightmare after all, it was instruction. It was prophecy.

Run and jump, Sal! Run and jump!

THREE

Mr. Nathan Steer
34 Magnolia Lane
Santa Rosa, CA 95405

Dear Mr. Steer:

Enclosed please find your manuscript
submission *Death Of a Football Player*. While
we have reviewed it with interest, we have
decided not to pursue it for representation.

The problem we have with the manuscript is
that while the subject—the bizarre manslaughter
of Peter Freeman, a Super Bowl football
personality—is intriguing, what you have
presented offers more questions than answers.
For example, you speculate why the young
woman, Jessie Malana, may have had reason to
kill him. You say that they had a conversation
while she was waitressing in the La Sangre
Saloon, but you can only speculate what was
said, and the cook either didn't hear or wouldn't
say what they talked about. Neither would

Corey Satori, who was also present. You further speculate that Mr. Freeman and Ms. Malana had a brief affair during that weekend he spent in La Sangre. You wonder if she was a woman scorned and as such ran over him with her car.

You refer to La Sangre as a religiously insular town, yet you have virtually no quotes from any of the townspeople themselves. Have you been able to locate any people who previously lived in La Sangre, who can shed some light on living in that town? Dr. Ralph Owen, the psychiatrist who summers in La Sangre, told the police that had treated Ms. Malana in Redding, CA, where he practiced and where she lived for several years, but again you only speculate on what she may have dealt with throughout her therapy. You say that in the California Highway Patrol's investigation, they were given access to Dr. Owen's records on Ms. Malana. While it's unlikely they would do so, have you at least asked the CHP if they—or even Dr. Owen himself—would release them to you? ?

Mr. Steer, we hope you're not discouraged. If you are able to get more information and more facts on the case, we would be willing to read a revised manuscript of *Death Of A Football Player*. You may also consider a less lurid title, as this title sounds more like a TV Movie-Of-The-Week.

In the meantime certainly feel free to submit your manuscript to other agencies and/or publishers. We wish you the best of luck with it.

Sincerely,

Cindy Carlton
San Francisco Writer's Agency

Nathan's wife, Julie, asked him why he'd kept that rejection letter taped to his desk for six months now. Was he a glutton for punishment? Nathan told her that every word of the letter was true, and it was a righteous punch in the jaw that he, ever the hopeful investigative journalist, certainly needed. After both his initial report of the La Sangre accident of Father's Day, June 17, 1984 *and* his follow-up two weeks later of the California Highway Patrol's investigation both hit the Associated Press wire, with his byline no less, he thought his career was made.

Instead, here he was sitting in his home office-cum-guest room on a Saturday night, trying to pound out a story on the Annual Santa Rosa Art Festival. His not-for-publication opener was "Yes folks, another bunch of delusionally talented bums who ought to just get a job tortured us with their 'art' at the Annual Santa Rosa Art Festival, at the Fairgrounds on Saturday."

His hostility was pure projection and he

knew it. The two AP pieces from a year ago that were next to the rejection letter looked ridiculous to him now. "Sheer luck," he admitted out loud for the first time, and at long last. "No talent, just sheer luck. I was just at the right place at the right time."

Julie would certainly disagree with that, but her opinion didn't count; she was his wife, wasn't much of a reader, and she would have thought his hardware store list was Pulitzer Prize material. She sure did love him though, with his thick glasses, big nose, and skinny body. He loved her too, her frizzy mousy hair and pear-shaped body, with a plentiful ass that he couldn't help but grab every time she walked by.

Julie was a nurse at Santa Rosa General Hospital, and brought home most of the bacon, including medical and dental benefits. "I'm a kept man," he half-joked to her and anyone else, although he did bring home a paycheck—however paltry—as Special Events Writer for the *Santa Rosa Dispatch*. "Stop it," she'd respond, "something will happen." But they were in their early 30s now and talking about kids. They were already struggling to pay the rent on their two-bedroom home in Old Town Santa Rosa. Maybe he'd have to use his office for the kids and get a real job. If they're going to buy a house, or a condo, they'd better get on it. Real estate in Sonoma County was steadily climbing.

"Sheer luck," he repeated.

A year ago he and Julie just happened to be driving north on CA Highway 1 early that Sunday morning, June 17 . They agreed on a casual Sunday drive up the coast, with breakfast at Bodega Bay or maybe even try the La Sangre Saloon for the first time. ("I doubt they're open until noon," Julie said. "I hear it's a very religious town.")

Still, they'd take a chance, and just before entering La Sangre from the south, they saw a black sports car, looked like a Maserati, tearing southbound and crashing into the guard rail. Nathan and Julie watched in horror as the female driver was ejected from the car and plummeted down the cliff to the ocean below.

Julie screamed. Nathan brought their Ford Bronco to a fast, safe stop, jumped out, and ran to the Maserati, its horn blaring. Looking over the guard rail he saw the young woman's broken and bloodied body on the rocks 70 feet below, being washed clean by the powerful waves. The body seemed to have lodged itself between two large rocks, so the waves couldn't pull it out to sea; the seagulls would have a feast if it wasn't removed quickly. He looked in the crumpled car, wanting to stop the horn's blasting, but decided not to touch anything. The seat belt was rolled up; she hadn't been wearing it.

Julie, who worked in the Emergency Room,

snapped into work mode as she hopped into the driver's seat of the Bronco and pulled it out of harm's way on the narrow winding road. She got out and joined Nathan at the guard rail. "She's dead?" Of course she knew the answer; she made a rhetorical question out of respect.

"Yeah. It's impossible to get down there from here."

"Nathan look!" A short ways up the road, within the town, was a man sitting in the middle of the road, holding another man in his arms, both of them bloodied. A tall, thin woman stood over them. A fourth person was lying on the steps of one of the buildings.

Nathan and Julie got back in the Bronco and drove ahead and got out, approaching the three people in the road. "We saw the car crash at the curve," he said to the woman who was standing over the two men. "The driver was ejected over the cliff, and I'm certain she's dead. Is that the same car that hit these two?"

"Yes," the woman nodded. "We know her. She lives...lived here."

"I'm a Registered Nurse," Julie offered. "Can I help?"

The woman had introduced herself as Lillian Walker, also a Registered Nurse and said "Sal," pointing to the man holding the body, "is all right, the blood on him is from the victim." Her voice caught briefly. "He's dead." She motioned over to the young man on the porch of the grocery store, who appeared calm. "That's Corey, Sal's son. He's got a broken left femur, it's being set by a doctor."

"What doctor?" Julie asked. No one else was there.

Lillian looked and then closed her eyes in response; she wasn't surprised.

Sal, still holding the body, called over to his son, "Corey? Are you all right?"

"Yeah Dad!" the kid cried back. "How's Pete?"

"It's no good Son," and the kid cried "NOOOO!" and burst into tears.

"Sal," Lillian said to him evenly, "I'm calling 9-1-1." He nodded, still holding onto Pete while she went into the grocery store for the phone.

Nathan and Julie stood by helplessly with the incessant blaring of the Maserati in the distance. Nathan squatted down and asked the man, Sal, what happened, but the man just cried "Oh Pete, I'm sorry!"

People began pouring out of the church a few hundred feet up the road, descending onto the scene, screaming and crying and praying. It was madness, hysteria. Like the seagulls, Nathan thought. All he and Julie could do was try to protect Sal, who wouldn't leave the body, from the small crowd that was praying and shouting "We have to lay hands on the football player to save him!" In the meantime Lillian came out of the grocery store after calling 9-1-1 and, shaking her head at the insanity, sat with Corey to wait for the police and the ambulance.

Nathan had witnessed accident scene madness before, but aggressive as he could be with a news story, he was also smart. Just hold back. Don't piss off the cops, and don't catch heat from the paper for intrusion. He'll just get his information from the police when they're ready to tell him something and call it into the paper. Besides, he'd already beat everyone else to it, he'll just wait for the cops to give him the story, his story. He already knows that the woman in the Maserati was a local, it could be personal vengeance. But the body...is that.... Nathan didn't follow football, but he recognized the face from all the public service announcements, especially Nancy Reagan's "Just Say No" Campaign. It was Pete Freeman of the San Francisco Forty-Niners.

Nathan's story hit the AP wire within a few hours, and *Nathan Steer - Investigative Reporter* was finally established and validated.

"Sheer luck!" Nathan said to himself now, exactly a year later.

It was 9 PM. Like pulling weeds in the yard, washing dishes, and doing laundry, Nathan knew the only way to get the art show piece done was to just bite the bullet and do it. He deleted his bitter opening sentence, and fought the temptation to make up more bitter openings. ("Once again, folks, Staff Writer Nathan Steer's talent for being in the right place at the right time has taken him to the Annual Santa Rosa Art Festival!")

The phone rang. Nathan grabbed it before it could wake Julie.

"Hello?"

"Nate!"

"Yeah Mitch." Mitch was a CB ham operator in Santa Rosa who monitored police calls and alerted Nathan of anything that sounded worthwhile.

Julie picked up the bedroom extension. "Hello?" She was groggy.

"I got it Hon," Nathan said.

"You better stay on, Julie," Mitch told her, "you'll both want to hear this." He knew Nathan liked Julie to be his second pair of ears whenever possible. "You're not going to believe this buddy, I hardly believe it myself."

"So tell me already."

"I'll tell you just as I heard it. 'I think someone is being killed at the cliff in La Sangre.' That's what the caller said."

"What? You mean a domestic assault?"

"I don't know. All I heard was someone

who identified herself as just Ruby said 'I think someone is being killed at the cliff in La Sangre.' A deputy's on his way now. You'd better do the same bud. I'm calling the San Francisco stations now, and they pay me a lot more than you do. They'll remember your story from last year, and you know they'll get there in a hurry, they might even scoop you."

Nathan kicked into gear. "Okay Mitch. I'm heading out, I'll call you when I get there."

"Good luck Nate."

"Thanks. Over and out."

"I don't believe this!" he said as he dashed into the bedroom to get dressed. Julie was already doing the same.

"Oh no Jules, it might not be anything. You know how crazy Ruby is."

"I know, but you can't take a chance, Nathan. I'm going."

"I was just being polite Hon, I hoped you would." He knew there was no way she'd miss out on this, even if she had to show up at the hospital in the morning with little or no sleep.

They didn't say anything until they were on the road leading from Santa Rosa to La Sangre, with Nathan avoiding the temptation to speed. It was a two-lane road with blind turns, and would be particularly blind once they hit the coastal fog.

Nathan broke their silence. "Last year, and now this. Does Father's Day make people in that town go crazy?"

"I don't know babe, but you're going to find out." She reached over and squeezed his arm.

Neither of them said what they were both thinking: there are no domestic disputes in La Sangre. Mitch had told them so last year, after the big tragedy. "I never heard a single Domestic Dispute call from La Sangre. They either don't have them, or that pastor-guy handles it." So, if this isn't a DD, it could be the break Nathan needed for his book.

"So Ruby just said 'Someone is being killed at the cliff in La Sangre,'" Julie mused. "You know Nathan, there really ought to be a fence along that cliff."

After a moment, he responded with chilling clarity. "A fence wouldn't help. The birds are attacking tonight. I know it."

Julie looked at her husband. He was serious. Was he speaking metaphorically, or was he being literal? She'd seen Nathan like this once before, a year ago in La Sangre, and she was afraid to ask, both then and now.

They reached Highway 1 by 9:20 and turned left for the two miles south to La Sangre.

"That's strange," Julie said.

"What?"

"No fog."

"You're right. Hey, grab the spotlight will

you? It's on the floor in the back, I'm sure it's charged."

Julie undid her seat belt and grabbed the LED spot. She clicked it on and off. "It's good."

Nathan slowed down just past the La Sangre Christian Church on the right that marked the beginning of town, and made a right onto the dirt road that led down to the small homes that dotted the bluff. A county deputy car was parked on the bluff at the end of the road, lights flashing, a small group surrounding it. Two deputies were standing 50 feet away at the edge of the cliff, pointing spotlights down to the ocean.

Nathan parked a respectful distance from the deputies' car and got out, grabbing his camera and spotlight.

"Look," Julie pointed at the small crowd. "There's Lillian." They ran up to her. (Just like last year, Julie remembered.)

"What are you two doing here?" Lillian asked, relieved to see them. She could use some friendly assistance.

"What happened Lillian?" Julie asked her.

"All we know is that some of us—the whole town maybe—heard somebody screaming 'You don't do that to children!' and then 'There's always one more!' It was loud, scary, even over the ocean. I called 9-1-1, but they said that Ruby, who lives in the closest house to where it happened, had already called in. I told the dispatchers I had no further information, so I found Ruby and asked her. She said after the screaming she heard a car tearing down Highway 1, to the south. A few others heard that too."

Nathan nodded and readied his camera. "Come on, let's go." He and Julie and Lillian quickly walked toward the edge of the cliff, a couple of townspeople following them.

"Hey, stand back!" one of the deputies shouted.

"Ron...Deputy Haver, it's Nathan Steer!"

"Oh Nate, yeah, come and take your photos. Remember, they belong to the Sheriff's Department until we release them back to you. And careful where you walk, all of you, we're going to be looking for footprints. Miss Walker, is that you?"

"Yes Deputy," Lillian replied.

"We need to keep everyone back. They'll listen to you. Tell them the sheriff is on his way, and an ambulance. Keep them back by our car."

"All right." She took Julie's arm to steer her and the few who followed back to the others. "Explain to them they're looking for footprints," she advised one of the men, "we can't be in the area."

"Careful Nathan!" Deputy Haver shouted as Nathan reached the edge of the cliff. Haver and the other deputy had gone as close to the edge as was safe and were scanning the rocks below. "There's a body down there." Haver didn't mean to say it so loud, because the small crowd heard him and gasped.

Nathan wasn't surprised. He moved in next to the deputies, steadied himself and shot a picture. The flash was actually more illuminating than the spotlights, however brief.

"Do you recognize him, Nathan?" Haver handed him binoculars and aimed the spotlight. "You're around here a lot."

"I...I can't tell! It looks like the body got wedged between the rocks, head first."

"Yeah," the other deputy said, "it shot into those rocks like an arrow."

"I see two legs, wearing jeans, and running shoes," Haver said. "Looks like a male. Can either of you tell the make of the shoes?"

"No."

"Me either."

"Bill," Ron said to his other deputy, "phone in and tell them we'll need help, maybe a rescue chopper. Explain the situation, they'll know which equipment to bring, maybe they'll repel off the cliff instead of the chopper, that's their decision. Nathan, go ask the townspeople if anyone is missing. There's only about a hundred people in this town."

Nathan ran back to Julie, where she and Lillian were successfully keeping the rubbernecking townspeople at bay. "The deputy is requesting," Nathan spoke loudly to the small crowd, "that you all check to see if anyone in your household is missing. Or if anyone living alone is missing."

A few people nodded and went toward the homes, then Nathan whispered to Julie and Lillian, "All they can see is what looks like a male body, wearing jeans and running shoes. They can't see what type of shoes." He ran back to the deputies.

"Lillian!" Julie suddenly had a horrible thought. "Where is Matthew?"

"He had to drive to Fresno to pick up a part. His car's still gone. He should be back soon."

"Lillian!" a woman ran toward her.

"Connie!" Foreboding struck Lillian. "Connie, where is Sal?"

"I...I don't know. We just had a big fight, and he left. Then I heard the screaming out here."

"What was Sal wearing?"

"What do you mean?"

"Connie," Lillian kept her voice level and professional, and came in close, gently grabbing her forearms. "Just tell me, what was Sal wearing when he left?"

Connie shook her head. "What...what he always wears, a polo shirt, he grabbed his jacket when he left. Jeans, his running shoes."

"What kind of running shoes, Connie?"

"What kind of...why?"

"Just tell me sweetie, what kind of shoes?"

"Nikes."

"Lillian!" another female voice cried out. It was Anne Owen, wife of Dr. Owen, running up to her. "Have you seen Ralph? No one else has!"

"Anne, come with me." Lillian steered her away from Connie towards Julie. "Anne, this is Julie Steer, we work together at the hospital. We're helping the deputies. She's just going ask you some questions." Lillian left them and went back to Connie. "Come on Connie, you can't leave your baby too long, let's go inside." She put her arm around Connie and guided her back to the house.

"Mrs. Owen," Julie asked her calmly, "can you tell me what your husband was wearing the last you saw him?"

"What? Just his dirty flannel shirt, jeans, running shoes. Why?"

"What kind of running shoes?"

"Oh those...Reeboks. Why?"

Ten minutes later Connie, Lillian, and Mrs. Owen sat in the Satoris' living room, waiting. Holding her sleeping baby helped Connie stay relatively calm.

The door opened suddenly and heavily. All three women jumped.

"Corey!" Connie almost screamed. "Corey!" She struggled to get up from the couch with the baby until Lillian took him from her. Connie ran and threw her arms around her son, in tears.

"Oh Corey, all this time! I've been so worried!"

Uncertain if or how to return the hug, Corey managed to put a hand on her back. "Mom," was all he could manage.

"Oh Corey, thank God! Both my children are here!"

"I got in a couple hours ago." Corey looked around the room.

"Hi Lillian." Then he looked at Mrs. Owen, wondering why she was there. She'd never been in their home before.

"Corey," Lillian asked, "did you talk to anyone outside?"

"Yeah, Deputy Haver wanted me and Doyle to tell them what we both heard."

"You two were in your rooms at the gas station?"

"Yeah, but I went to sleep early, I didn't hear anything until the sirens. Doyle's outside helping the deputies, but he was asleep too. Lillian, what the *hell* is going on?"

"I'm going to make some coffee," Mrs. Owen announced and went into the kitchen, finding solace in duty.

"Thank you, Anne," Lillian tried to establish some kind of order. "Everybody else just sit down."

"I don't *want* to sit down," Corey said, his voice raising, "and I don't want any goddamn coffee. Just tell me what is going on! Someone outside said there's a body at the bottom of the cliff!" Corey looked around. "So where is Sal in the middle of all this?"

Lillian took a breath and nodded. "The deputies called an emergency rescue team so they can get to the bottom of the cliff and retrieve the body. All we know is that it looks like a man's body, wearing jeans and running shoes."

"Yeah, they told me that. But they wouldn't tell me who it is."

"Corey," his mother asked him, "we told the deputies that your father always wears Nikes."

Corey nodded, then he understood. "What kind of shoes are..." he faltered.

"They can't tell from here," Lillian answered. "Dr. Owen was also wearing jeans and running shoes, Reeboks. Nobody knows where he or your father are."

Corey looked around him: at Lillian, the unofficial second in command of La Sangre after Sal; he looked at his mother, who had lied to him all his life about his real father; at Mrs. Owen, wife of Dr. Ralph Owen, Psychiatrist. "And you all wonder why," he took a step back and announced to them all in disgust, "I left this town last year and never came back? You actually *wonder* that? Mom? This place is sick, and I knew it and got the hell out! Corey Satori, the 'Pastor's Son,' has left La Sangre. 'Elvis has left the building.' And the minute I'm back you give me this horror story about an unidentified body at the bottom of the cliff, that may be..." his throat caught. No, he wasn't going to let his guard down here, not in the house he grew up in, and certainly not in front of his lying mother. Nothing had changed in the past year. Not a god damn thing had changed!

"Corey, please," Lillian pleaded, still holding the baby.

"Please *what*?"

"I...I want you to meet someone. Please, Corey, I'm going to hand him to you. But sit down first."

Confused, angry, and unable to fight back the tears he swore wouldn't happen, Corey resignedly flopped on the couch and looked at Lillian with the baby. "Is that your baby?" he asked Lillian. But he knew who it was. His grandmother Grace had told him.

"No Corey, I want you to meet your little brother, Freeman Satori. He's three months old."

Corey wanted to stay angry, it was all he had, and yet his arms involuntarily reached up as he received the warm, soft baby from Lillian. The baby looked up at Corey, knowingly, it seemed.

Connie watched her two children, her two sons, the immediate natural love between them. Everything is going to be okay, she tried to believe. Oh please God.

Mrs. Owen managed to get the coffee maker

going, while Lillian and Connie sat and watched the anger and tears on Corey's face melt into wonder at his little brother.

They were all waiting to find out whose body was at the bottom of the cliff, and as they waited, they had plenty of time to think about everything that happened the past year.

Had it only been a year? So much had happened since then it seemed longer.

JULY - AUGUST, 1984

FOUR

**HEROIC DEATH OF RETIRED
NFL PLAYER PETER FREEMAN
RULED ACCIDENTAL**
by Nathan Steer
Santa Rosa Dispatch Staff Writer

LA SANGRE, California (AP) July 1, 1984. The death of retired San Francisco 49ers running back Peter Freeman in an auto vs. pedestrian incident was an accident, according to the report from the California Highway Patrol. Freeman, 34, was pronounced dead at the scene on June 17 in La Sangre, California, a small coastal town located 85 miles north of San Francisco. Witnesses described seeing Freeman run into the middle of California State Route 1 and push Corey Satori, 17, out of the way of a speeding black 1976 Maserati. Satori suffered a broken leg and contusions when he hit a post of the general store, and Freeman was run over by the vehicle.

Witnesses identified the driver of the vehicle as Jessie Malana, 24, a temporary La Sangre resident originally from Redding, California. Moving at a dangerously high rate of speed in the

15 mph zone, Malana continued driving down the road after striking Freeman, ultimately hitting a cliff side guard rail and catapulting to her death below. The autopsy on Malana revealed no sign of physical impairment and the toxicology report showed no trace of drugs nor alcohol. She was not wearing a seat belt.

Pete Freeman retired from football in 1982 after helping the San Francisco 49ers win its first NFL championship game by defeating the Cincinnati Bengals in Super Bowl XVI. *Sports Illustrated* announced it will honor Freeman on the cover of its next issue, the fourth time Freeman has appeared on the cover.

Nathan had scotch-taped the piece alongside his first AP piece that had appeared in the late Father's Day Sunday editions. During the two weeks between the accident and the CHP report, Nathan had investigated—all right snooped—through La Sangre, trying to get information from anyone who would be willing to talk to him.

But nobody would. The best he could get was "The Pastor advised us only to talk to the police. No reporters." The worst he got was outright hostility of stares and slamming doors. All he could garner was that his initial hunch was right: there was definitely something wrong with that town. There was some dark secret that he was determined to uncover.

"Hey!"

Nathan jumped. "I told you not to do that!"

"Oh *sooorry*," Julie rolled her eyes from the doorway, "but you weren't writing, babe, you were gloating over your Associated Press news clippings."

"Well that, but I was also thinking: do you remember how weird all those people were acting, at the accident?"

"You mean the praying, running around and laying hands on everyone and everything?"

"Yeah, and shouting about getting Satan the hell out of town."

Julie came into the room and sat on the sleeper sofa. "Nathan, it happens all the time at the hospital, I've told you that. People come in and lay their hands on the sick, they pray in strange languages. And yes, they've often said 'I rebuke you Satan!' when referring to the infirmity. It's harmless and if it makes the patient and the families feel better, fine. The doctors don't mind, except for restricted cases, as long as they don't get too loud."

Nathan swiveled around to face her. "Yeah, but at La Sangre, that morning, it seemed so..." he wrinkled his nose.

"Extreme?"

He pointed at her and nodded.

"Maybe so," Julie shrugged. "Oh! This may interest you, I meant to tell you. An application was just submitted to the hospital, for work in the ER. It hit the nurse gossip chain like brush fire. It's from Lillian Walker, the nurse from La Sangre, remember her?"

Nathan's eyes widened. "I sure do. She, Pastor Satori and his son Corey were the only town witnesses, besides us and that shrink and his wife who had just driven in from the north. Walker and Satori also seemed to be leaders of the town. They were polite but they stonewalled me, and they've been doing it for the past two weeks."

"Nathan, would it help you if she got hired at the hospital?"

"Yeah babe! I'm sure she'd get hired with your recommendation. You saw her profession-al behavior that day regarding the victims. She set that kid's leg, didn't she?"

"No, she said it was done by some doctor, 'a big guy with a red beard.'"

"Yeah, that's what Satori said, and then this supposed doctor disappeared into thin air." Nathan considered for a moment. "I don't know Jules, now that I think about it, maybe it's not a good idea. She could be as crazy as the towns-people. I don't think I'd want some crazy-lady attaching a catheter to me."

"I don't know, Nathan, I think she's all right. We spent much of that day together. That mys-tery doctor must be some kind of cover-up, maybe she didn't want the Nurse's Registry to smack her for setting a bone. But I think her medical ability and people skills are fine."

Nathan considered. "Well?"

Julie chuckled. "I'll talk to my friend in personnel. But, if you get an article out of this..."

"A book."

"...a *book* out of this, I want an acknowledgment."

"You got it."

SANTA ROSA GENERAL HOSPITAL
EMPLOYEE NEWSLETTER
JULY 1984

We here at SRGH are pleased to welcome Lillian Walker, R.N., to our staff. Nurse Walker was born in Santa Rosa and raised in nearby La Sangre. After graduating from Santa Rosa High School, she moved to Seattle, where she received her Nursing Degree from The Seattle School of Nursing. Afterward she worked in Seattle General Hospital in the ER. "I loved Seattle," she says, "but I think I got tired of all the rain." Nurse Walker moved back to La Sangre in 1970, where she has worked as a resident nurse and caregiver for the town. Her hobbies include long walks along Highway 1 ("It's my prayer and thinking time"), reading, and church activities. "The people of La Sangre are like a family, I depend on them, they depend on me, and that's nice. It's nice to be needed." Nurse Walker has been assigned to the ER, and we all welcome her.

Connie missed her period. The last time that happened was her senior year in high school, after she and Peter Freeman had...made love in a lonely field outside of Bakersfield. Otherwise she could set her watch by her periods.

She was both surprised and hopeful. Ever since that night, the night before the accident, she and Sal had made love nearly every single night, and some mornings and afternoons, a far cry from their couple-of-times-a-month during their entire marriage. In their newfound lovemaking, a different Sal emerged: lustful, grateful, and joyous. It took her a while to stop questioning it and to just relax and enjoy it. She tried to obliterate the one time he cried out Jessie's name, that first time. It was just a slip, an overflow from his adulterous relationship with that girl that was just two hours fresh. Typical man. After all, Connie reasoned, she's lucky she'd never cried out "Peter!" Or had she?

Anyway, she'll wait for another cycle before she goes to the doctor. In the meantime their marriage was on a new...what, road? Plateau? Were they getting better, growing together, really getting to know each other? They were touching each other more often. At night in bed, he loved to lay on his side against her back, his right arm over her, his hand cupping her breast. He always fell asleep before she did.

Sal sat alone in the church. He'd started having nightmares, and he knew their source. The California Highway Patrol could say "accidental death" as many times as they wanted, but he—with Doyle and Mary the Operator as his henchmen—knew the truth. Doyle and Mary could stupidly claim "It was God's will" all they wanted, but Sal knew it was his own fault.

So, what are you going to do about it, Sal?

"I DON'T KNOW!" his cry echoed through the empty church. "I JUST DON'T KNOW!"

Dr. Ralph Owens and his wife Anne were sitting on their front porch in their rockers, enjoying the ocean with its sound and breeze, a world away from dry, flat Redding, California. But neither of them liked the seagulls; those pests—flying rats they were—seemed to have nothing better to do than just survive and procreate, at least that's what Ralph said. Anne didn't just dislike the seagulls, she was afraid of them. These birds seemed to be able to hear and see everything that happened in this town, and gossip to each other about it.

"I don't like them."

"The seagulls again dear?" Ralph smiled and pulled out his pipe. "It's been an upsetting two weeks. Jessie's death..."

"Do you think that's all it was? A simple death? You heard what Nurse Lillian and the

Pastor said, that she was driving way too fast to make that hairpin curve, and *without* a seat belt. And she was trying to hit that boy, Corey. What was going on in her mind?"

Everything his wife said was true, her question legitimate. It never ceased to amaze Ralph how, with her average intelligence, she was a good sounding board for him. It was that way since he was in med school and she was an undergrad at UC San Francisco, where they met, dated, got pregnant, married, and she dropped out to raise the family.

"I told the CHP that I had been treating her in Redding, dealing with her rage," Ralph said. "But I never thought she'd explode like that. I thought several months by the seaside would help her, it's historically therapeutic. We had a house sitting here, the girl had no money, the Pastor gave her a job as a waitress in the Saloon. I still had sessions with her by phone, we'd meet in Sacramento once a month when you and I went down. She was doing well. Professionally I thought, and still think, that it was a good idea. Maybe our owning the home she rented..."

"We didn't charge her rent."

"Well, maybe her *staying* in our home might be seen as a conflict, but I don't think so. Remember I asked my lawyer, he didn't see how it could be considered coercion; unless we had questionable material lying around, besides *The*

Joy Of Cooking."

Anne shook her head, ignoring his playful jab. "There's just something about this town that might have affected her."

"Honey, we've always known these people are religious fanatics. They're harmless, I told Jessie that. But she started going to their church, to their Bible studies...."

"Well?"

Dr. Owen looked at her. "You think that..."

"She was brainwashed."

He grimaced. "Jessie was too smart for that, she was a free thinker, and I should know. No, she did it to herself."

"Whatever 'it' means. Ralph, I want to find out."

"Find out, meaning what?"

"Find out if the people here can brainwash a vulnerable young woman..."

"Jessie Malana may have been damaged, but she was far from vulnerable to the world at large."

"Well, I'm going to do some sleuthing."

"And just how are you going to do that, Sherlock? That kid from the Santa Rosa paper..."

"Nathan Steer."

"...he got nowhere with anyone here, not even with us. So how are you going to do it?"

"I'm going to start attending their church." She turned to face Ralph. "And you're going with me."

Ralph was taken aback. This was a first. Neither of them was ever religious; they raised their two kids the same way. Their atheist daughter was teaching philosophy and religion at UC Berkeley, their musician son in LA had found religion in dead rock stars. ("Dad, I'm telling you that Jim Morrison is *alive!*") Viewing all this, Ralph could only respond with "I think I'd rather finish reading Ayn Rand's *Atlas Shrugged.*"

"Oh you're never going to finish that book." Anne looked at him with purpose. "No Ralph, I mean it. I'm going to that church and I want you to come with me."

Ralph gave her his honey-you've-got-to-be-kidding look.

"I'm serious," Anne persisted. "You've been talking about writing a book, some kind of book. 'Publish or perish' they tell you, don't they?"

"Oh Annie, that's what they tell college professors, not doctors."

"Are you kidding? All of the top shrinks are writing books about dysfunctional people, dysfunctional communities. Just think what a book La Sangre would make. And you actually live here, right in the middle of it!"

A nearby seagull squawked.

Have you heard? That psychiatrist's wife, Anne Owen, had the nerve to ask me when the women's Bible studies meet. Really? The nerve

of that atheist! She's actually married to a psychiatrist, and they're the devil's spawn. Yes, I
know, they certainly are, and I have proof. Do
you remember on that day when Satan was trying to take over the town, when we heard that
Jessie girl's black sports car crash up, and she
had run over that football player? Yes, I remember, what about it? Didn't you notice when we
heard the noise and came running out of the
church, that the psychiatrist and his wife had
just pulled over, coming back into town in that
big fancy car of theirs, a Cadillac or something.
Well, they pulled over and were just watching it.
Just sitting there watching it. Now wait a minute Mary, he did get out and run over to help; he
jumped out right away and ran up to where the
Pastor and Nurse Walker were, along with that
nosy reporter and his wife. Well yes, but I'll bet
he was gleeful, like he thought 'Oh good, mis-
sion accomplished.' Yes, I suppose you're right.
Well, should we let her into our women's Bible
study? Of course we should. If we could get her
saved, think of what a coup that would be! And
maybe the psychiatrist himself will start going to
the men's Bible studies, and he'll be saved too!
Wouldn't that be wonderful? He'll denounce his
satanic psychiatry and turn to the Lord for healing. Then he can tell all the other psychiatrists
about his salvation, and they too will stop doing
Satan's work. Hallelujah!

FIVE

July 15, 1984

Mrs. Connie Satori
General Delivery
La Sangre, CA 94923

Dear Connie,

It's hard for me write this letter, but it would have been harder for me to call you on the phone about what I have to say, or rather what I have to ask. So I thought I'd use this letter to break the ice on my request.

First of all, I can't begin to tell you how much it has meant to me, how much it has helped me, to meet you and your husband, and of course Peter's son, Corey, my grandson. I am hesitant to refer to Corey as such, not that he isn't my grandson, of course, but because I don't want to in any way infringe upon your or your husband's relationship with Corey. After all you two raised him, and obviously did a wonderful job at it, and for that I'm very grateful. Still, I would love to continue having Corey, and you, in my life. The main reason is, of course, that he's the child of my only son, Peter, and it's keeping him alive for me.

Now, there is Peter's considerable estate to discuss, and Corey is his only child. But as you can understand I need time before I can deal with all that. In the meantime, I want to do what I can for Corey, and what you'll allow me to do. I would love to talk in person, or at least on the phone. I don't want to add any more confusion to Corey's life than what I'm sure he's already going through, but perhaps I can make his new life somewhat easier for him. Helping Corey would also make my own new life as a widow easier for me.

Please let me know when you would be willing to talk. We exchanged phone numbers when we met last month before Peter's funeral, and I hope we can talk soon.

Sincerely,
Grace Freeman

"Corey, are you sure you want to go to Bible College?"

"Well," he hesitated too long, "yeah, sure I do."

Corey and his mother were standing at the

cliff. Connie folded her arms, just in an effort to make herself more physically comfortable. She really ought to talk to Sal about putting some park benches here. Every home had some kind of view of the ocean, from their porches and decks. But benches at the cliff would be nice. Standing up always seemed to rush conversation.

"I just want to make sure, Corey," she gathered her thoughts. "It's been a month since the... accident...and we all had knee jerk reactions to it. Your father is in self loathing, he feels totally responsible for both Jessie and Peter's deaths."

"And well he should!" Corey turned toward her. "And you Mom, are you having your own self-loathing?"

Connie met his gaze, and shamed herself by turning away, back to the ocean. "Yes. Yes I am."

Corey raised his voice. "Why didn't you *tell* me?"

"You mean that Peter Freeman was your real father?"

"Hello? Yes!"

"Please Corey. I already told you that I was going to wait until you were 18, this September, before I told you, and told Peter. He's...he was... wealthy and famous. They probably gossip in the sports world as much as they do in Hollywood. 'Super Bowl Winner Has Love Child!' Maybe not, I don't know. I just wanted Peter to know that I wanted nothing from him while your father..."

"'Sal,' you mean."

Connie lowered her head. This conversation was late in coming, probably too late. "I hope you won't call him that."

"I can't promise that, but it's hard for me to call him 'Dad' now."

"But that part isn't your Dad...isn't Sal's fault. Even he didn't know Peter was your father. I was the one who decided not to tell him, or you. I'm the only one who's at fault."

"Well then, can you blame me for being angry?'

Connie exhaled, aware she'd been holding her breath through this exchange. "No Corey, of course I can't. And saying sorry isn't enough, I know. I just made what I thought was the right decision." She turned back to Corey, and his eyes were still on her, intent, pursuant, angry. She wasn't used to this, it was never supposed to happen this way. Corey was all she had, and now she was losing him too. She still hadn't gotten her period; she was pretty sure she was pregnant. Was she going to have to go through this again? What mistakes is she going to make? Is that all a mother does, make mistakes?

"Listen to me, Corey. I think it's time for you to get away, just like we talked, the morning that Peter..."

"My father," Corey corrected her curtly.

"Yes, your father, came into town. Before he

arrived, you and I talked right here, and then you walked away without even a see-you-at-lunch Mom..."

"Oh yeah, lunch at the Saloon, when Pete came in and Sal...Mom, don't ask me to call him Dad."

Connie started.

"Oh all right, I can say it directly to him if I have to, but I can't look at him—when Pete came in and Sal shoved us out of the Saloon. What was *that* about? Did Sal know something, about you and Pete? Are you going to lie to me some more?" He choked off the last sentence and turned away.

"No Corey! Your father knew nothing more than I got pregnant by a boy in high school, that's all he knew! Now please, listen to me! I talked on the phone with Peter's mother yesterday, Grace. She wants to help you out financially, and it comes from a good heart, not out of any kind of obligation. I like her, I trust her. With Peter's standing in the UCLA Alumni Association, she can bypass the acceptance deadline and get you into UCLA."

Corey looked at her. "I didn't respond to UCLA's acceptance because I thought I'd be a good Christian boy and go to Bible college and become a pastor like my—like the man I thought was my father—so I can run a church and live with lies, like the rest of this goddamn town."

Connie gasped.

"Yes, like the 'goddamn bastard,'" Corey continued, voice raising, "that Sal called me that day when Pete my *real father* came into the saloon. Well, the 'goddamn bastard' is finally speaking up!" It had be to said, and he wasn't sorry he said it. But he didn't gloat about it either, softening almost immediately. "I'm sorry Mom, I really am, but I'm disgusted, and you can't blame me for that."

"No Corey, no I can't." She searched for a way to get back to where they were, where they used to be with each other. "Maybe we'd better talk about this in a couple days, before we go too far." But they already had. It was too late to go back. She was sure she lost him.

"Look Mom," Corey made an attempt, "Monterey Bible College has that prep thing in August that I'm set up for, where new students stay at the campus for three days to get acclimated, talk with professors, discuss their classes. Let's go ahead with that. Dad already..." he stopped himself, and had to chuckle. "Yeah all right, Dad, my 'father,' already paid for it. Why don't I go ahead with that, and then we'll see."

"And what about UCLA? Grace Freeman..."

"My grandmother," Corey corrected her.

Connie was taken aback, yet again. She supposed she'd have to get used to this. "Yes," she nodded, "your grandmother needs to know."

Corey knew when enough was enough. "I'm sorry Mom. This is all so...new. Can she hold off for a few days, at least until after I check out Monterey Bible College, see how I feel about it?"

"I'll ask her about the deadline. She didn't give me a date, but since UCLA starts in late September, we might be okay." Connie impulsively reached out for Corey but stopped herself, her left hand in mid-air. Corey softly grasped her hand and they watched the ocean together for a minute, holding hands.

I think he still loves me, Connie dared to hope.

She just wasn't so sure about Sal.

Sal sat alone, yet again, in the La Sangre Christian Church. He had prayed intently for what felt like two hours, although he was sure it wasn't that long. Never enough, it's never enough. He could pray for days and all he'd hear is the ocean, with the seagulls shrieking overhead.

Come on Sal, cut yourself some slack. Your prayers come from the heart, at least now they do, instead of from your own agenda. So what have you learned, up to this point?

Well, I felt good about my sermon—*our* sermon—last Sunday. I really thought my heart was open. I can't remember the last time I cried, in front of the congregation no less. But I don't care.

Those tears, they came from the heart too.

But will my tears wash away this guilt that's inside me? It's eating me up. And those nightmares I'm having? Is that really you speaking to me?

It is.

Okay, what about the "run and jump" thing that Jay's telling me to do?

You'll figure it out, Son. Do another sermon this Sunday like you did, just keep moving ahead in that direction. It'll all come together in time.

How much time?

Be patient.

Lillian was pleased that she was assigned to the ER under Julie Steer's training. They'd kept in touch since "that day" two months ago, even though Lillian was not at all cooperative with Julie's husband, Nathan, telling him politely more than once "I'm sorry Mr. Steer, I can't help you with your book." But it didn't stop a friendship from blossoming between the two women.

"Now that you've got the job with Santa Rosa General," Julie had asked her over the phone, "are you going to keep living in La Sangre? You told me you don't have a car."

But Lillian had in fact just bought herself a car, a bright yellow Toyota, and quickly brought her long-lost driving skills back up to par while commuting on the windy road between La

Sangre and Santa Rosa.

"But why do you live in that town?" Julie had persisted. "Those people are so...well, weird, and you're not that way at all!"

Lillian replied, simply, "I belong there." Which Julie didn't understand at all, and Lillian barely understood it herself, she just knew she had to be there, for whatever reason. Was she still hiding from life?

But the two women liked each other, and Lillian needed a friend, since the accident—she hated calling it that but there was no other word for it—had put a damper on the friendship she thought she was developing with Connie.

Connie and Sal were going through some-thing major, Lillian knew; the whole town was for that matter, due to the tabloid attention La Sangre was getting with wild rumors and specu-lation not since the Patty Hearst kidnapping in Berkeley of ten years ago. But as far as Connie was concerned, Lillian thought it best just to re-main available to her, whenever she wanted to talk.

In the meantime, Lillian and Julie went off to buy Lillian's nursing uniforms and shoes. Julie also helped Lillian pick out some street clothes that she thought would make good use of her tall, thin frame. "I know how to make clothes work for us ladies who may not have perfect figures," Julie advised her. "Look at these hips

I have to hide! I won't wear a girdle, and Nathan hates them!"

"Who wears girdles now? I wore falsies until I had my first boyfriend at 19, who convinced me to toss them."

So they were girlfriends together, chatting and laughing, even giggling, and they used it at work, especially in the ER, where their light-hearted exchanges with the variously trauma-tized patients eased the environment, relaxing the patients into knowing that, yes, they're going to be well taken care of here in the ER, these two nurses are here to help you, and if we can all find something humorous in it, we will. Most of the patients did indeed respond well, often with pained chuckles, to the girls' appropriate gai-ety. Julie and Lillian soon became known as the "Laverne and Shirley of Santa Rosa General."

So when the ambulance brought in an un-conscious man who had been electrocuted close to death, just weeks after Lillian had started, the two ladies went to work as if he could hear them.

"We know you can hear us," Julie said to the patient after the emergency team lifted him from the gurney onto the examination table, "and I think you're going to be all right. I'm Julie, and this is my sidekick, Lillian, and you're stuck with us as your two beautiful nurses."

Lillian stopped short at the man's face. She knew him: that well-weathered, world-weary face, the masculine creases that bordered his cheeks were even deeper now, and even in an unconscious state, his lips were in a playful grin.

No, it couldn't be. It wasn't until they had him completely stripped down and Lillian saw the hard, lean-muscled hairless body, not an ounce of fat on this mid- to late-fifties man, that she was sure she knew him. And what closed the deal was when she saw his...yes, *that*.

"Matthew!"

Julie looked at her. "You know him?" she whispered.

Lillian nodded as they turned him over to check for trauma on his backside. "Yes, definitely," she whispered back.

"You mean this is the Matthew from Seattle that you..."

The doctor took over. "Okay," he said to the two nurses, "he's coming out of it."

"I know him, Doctor," Lillian told him, controlling her sudden confusion.

"Good, get him talking."

Lillian put her face within inches of Matthew's. "Matthew, can you hear me? It's me, Lillian."

Matthew's eyes took a few seconds to open and focus—those damned beautiful blue eyes—and his lips—God those beautiful lips—spread and turned up at the edges.

"Lilly."

SIX

Sal knocked on the Owens' door, trying to remember the last time he had reached out to Dr. and Mrs. Owen. It was when he and Connie and Corey had moved to La Sangre 13 years ago, and the three of them—Corey always a well-behaved child—came by to introduce themselves and invite them to church. It was brief, but the Owens were both polite, even warm, with smiles of gratitude for the welcome basket and a kind explanation that we're not church-goers, we're just here for the summer. In the fall we may rent the cottage out, in the meantime, thank you for welcoming us.

"Well good morning Pastor Satori," Anne Owen now greeted him. "Is...is anything wrong? I mean..."

"No, I know, Mrs. Owen. We're all trying to get through, trying to understand, what happened last month."

"Has it been a month?" She shook her head. "It doesn't feel like it.

Sal nodded. "I know what you mean." He

looked over Anne's shoulder. "I'd like to have a few minutes with Dr. Owen, if he's available, that is."

"Oh of course Pastor, do come in."

Sal stepped inside the familiar living room, checking his memory at the door of that one night, just over a month ago, in this house with Jessie.

"Ralph?" Anne called. He came out of the second bedroom wearing a flannel shirt and jeans, barefoot. Sal had never considered it before, but this man—taller than Sal, beefy, well-balded, clean-shaven, and in good shape for a fifty-something—was a refreshing contrast to the stereotypically short psychiatrists with a Vandyke beard and German accent.

"Well, Pastor Satori, hello. What can I do for you?" Ralph immediately discerned a softer countenance in the Pastor than his usual tough-guy stance, as if he was always entering the ring.

"Doctor, I wonder if we can talk in private? It's a personal matter."

"Of course! I use the second bedroom as an office. Anne, would you bring us some coffee?"

Sal hesitated. "Oh, well..."

"I just brewed some fresh," she said, "or would you rather tea?"

"Oh no, coffee's fine, thank you."

Anne nodded and went into the kitchen.

"Come on back," Ralph led the way. It was

indeed an office, soothing in browns and greens, with two relaxing pastoral oil paintings on the wall. There was a desk, and two comfortable-looking easy chairs. Dr. Owen motioned Sal to one of the chairs.

"No psychiatrist couch?" Sal tried to break the ice, then realized that if anything, it was the doctor's responsibility to do that. Sal was so used to doing it himself with his own congregation during counseling.

"No, no couch. Oh, I have one in my office in Redding, but I don't use it much, never offer it to a patient unless it's necessary. Facing each other is more productive, I find. Please, sit."

"Thank you." Sal sat down, wondering what other light thing he could say to fill time until Mrs. Owen came in with the coffee.

But she returned quickly with a tray, prepared as if Sal, or somebody, was expected. "I'll let you gentlemen help yourself." She set the tray on the desk.

"Thank you dear," Ralph said. She nodded and left, shutting the door behind her.

"Cream or sugar?" Ralph asked.

"A dash of cream, thank you."

Ralph fixed Sal's coffee and handed it to him. He took his own black and sat down across from Sal, noting that Sal had his legs crossed in the "4" position, an understandable defense for a first-timer.

Sal took a sip of his coffee. It was strong and rich, much better than the La Sangre Saloon's, and even better than Connie's. "Good coffee," he said.

Ralph took a sip of his and set his mug down. He looked at Sal and asked, simply, "What's up?"

Sal held onto his mug, warming his hands. "Well Doctor, I'll admit I've never done this before."

"Neither have I."

"You mean 'Did you hear the one about the preacher who went to see a shrink?'"

Dr. Owen chuckled. "Yes, exactly." Good sense of humor for a preacher.

"Well Doctor, I'm actually here for someone else."

"A 'friend?'" Ralph gave his professional half-smile of letting the patient know that he knew.

"No, really," Sal responded, not minding the gentle *sure*-you-are. "It's for someone in my congregation. You know Doyle Seeno, the man who runs the gas station?"

"I can't say that I know him. Oh, I know *who* he is, from the gas station, but I'm sorry to say he's outright hostile to me, and to Mrs. Owen, which I don't appreciate."

"I'll have to apologize for him." Sal searched for the right words to say about Doyle, and suddenly Doyle wasn't his chief concern. "I feel like..." He couldn't avoid Dr. Owen's kind, professional countenance, the gentle eye contact. "I'm sorry, this is two separate worlds colliding, like our President who was once a movie star."

Ralph gave a hearty laugh. "I know what you mean. But I'm glad you came by. Oh, and for the record, the first hour is free."

"Thank you Doctor."

"You know, we're both professionals. Why don't you call me Ralph."

"I'd like that," Sal nodded. "Thank you Ralph. I'm Sal."

Dr. Owens extended his hand. "It's nice to finally get to know you, Sal."

Doyle woke up screaming, as he was doing almost nightly, increasing in frequency and intensity since the accident over a month ago. He was now alone above the gas station, in his room, after that football player had bunked with Corey in room across the hall, just that one night, the night before the accident. After that Corey moved back into his parents' home, saying he never wanted to set foot in that room again. But maybe the reason Corey no longer wanted to stay here was he didn't want to hear his screams at night, and Doyle couldn't blame him.

Worse, that same night, Satan had made Doyle run to the Pastor's house like a madman, with the false accusation that the football player had sex with Corey. Doyle knew in his heart it wasn't true, it came from Satan, who had possessed him. After Doyle told Pastor Satori the lie, Satan then had Doyle run through town, knocking on doors, screaming "Satan is taking over La Sangre!" And even "Satan has taken over the Pastor!" It wasn't Doyle doing that, it was Satan using him!

"Oh God!" Doyle pleaded now. "If you love me, help me!"

The townspeople were gossiping, but since they prefaced everything with "We really have to pray about..." and then filled in the juicy information, they didn't consider it gossip.

We really have to pray about Doyle. Really, what about? Well, Mary was working late at the grocery store last night, and she heard Doyle from his room above the gas station, screaming like a madman. Oh poor Doyle, he's such a good Christian but he just doesn't have any spiritual gifts, and certainly no discernment. I don't know about that, remember how well Doyle took over the Sunday service the morning of the accident when that sinful Jessie girl ran over that football player? Well, don't forget that if God can use an ass to speak to Balaam, he can use Doyle too. (Gasp!) Oh, it's all right to use the a-word, because it's in the Bible. Oh that's right, Numbers 22. But besides Doyle, we really have to pray about our Pastor too. What about? About that sermon he gave last Sunday? Oh, you mean where he quoted Matthew Chapter 7? Wasn't that something! How *dare* he ask that we all look into *our* own hearts as Christians! Oh, I know what you mean, as if *we* might be sinners at heart. Yes! After all, we don't drink or smoke or dance or go to movies, we're not sinners. Oh, speaking of movies, my daughter, Ruth, she's 14 now, she wanted to see that movie "Footloose," about a nice Christian town and some fool comes into town and tries to get the kids to start dancing! No! Was it rated R? I think so. You didn't let her go, did you! No of course not, it's just like your son, Jacob, remember when he wanted that game for Christmas a few years ago, what was it, "Masters Of The Universe?" Oh I remember, I wouldn't let him have that. I told him there's only one Master of the Universe, and that's our God! And oh he cried, he really wanted that evil game, but I told him it's for his own good. Well, that's why you shouldn't have a TV, children see those things on the TV. By the way, ever since that Satanic attack on our town on Father's Day, what about all those people who come into town now on weekends, snooping around and snapping photos? Well you know, the Pastor needs to put an end to that. Well, I talked to him about it, but he just said to leave them be, they're not trespassing. But I even see them going into the church, and you *know* they aren't Christians! Well, the Pastor needs to start locking the church doors. And that reminds me, did you notice how the Pastor is now preaching the grace message? Oh yes, I know about that grace message, it's where our sins are already forgiven, so now you can just go out and do whatever you want. Yes, that's right, and now he's preaching that! He's forgotten that fire and brimstone are the cornerstone, it's what keeps us on the narrow path. You're absolutely right. It's a long, slippery slope to hell, and good old fashioned fiery preaching is what people need to hear. Amen to that!

Lillian couldn't wait for her shift to end so she could visit Matthew in his hospital room, where they were keeping him for observation for the night. She was nervous and excited and angry and resentful. This was the day she'd long dreamed about, a lifelong fantasy, where she would tear this man apart, a man ten years her senior who took advantage of her youth and naivety in Seattle 27 years ago. Yes, she had counted every single one of those years!

And dammit, he *still* looked good, even better than ever, and as a patient in the ER no less, if all that was possible. How *dare* he not age the way she had! He still had that sleekness, that worldly knowing face with the properly accented lines, and oh that body! She knew every inch of it and she loved it. And what about in the ER when he opened his eyes and simply said "Lilly." He's the only one who ever called her that. Just saying her name, the sparkle in his eyes, his alley cat instincts...how *dare* he move her that way, how *dare* he stir her feelings, how *dare* he ignite her responses! Men like him can put the women's movement back a hundred years!

"Hi Matthew," she greeted him as neutrally as she could, void of any emotion one way or the other. To the attending nurse's aid who was just finishing up, she said "Please don't disturb us until I notify the floor station." The young aid nodded and left, closing the door behind her. Lillian walked over to his bed, not four feet from him with his Cheshire Cat smile.

"Lilly. It's so nice to see you again. Strange way to do it, I guess. I'm glad you continued with your nursing."

How *dare* he speak to her like that! So damned *familiar*! Here he was laid up in a hospital bed, the back raised 45 degrees, but she was the nurse. She was supposed to be in the power position, not him, not that lean version of Robert Mitchum who operated the Wild Mouse roller coaster at the 1962 Seattle World's Fair, where she thought she fell in love with him and spent the entire six-month run of the Fair with him, in his cheap hotel room and in the sleazy bars along the Seattle waterfront; the occasional days off they took together, driving up to Canada or down along the Columbia River from Portland to the ocean. How *dare* he!

"Why did you do it, Matthew?" Lillian finally asked. Yes, that was good, she used the right tone, she wasn't pleading. It was the power tone of a woman in control.

"Do what, Lilly?"

"'Do *what*? You said you would take me on the road with you, follow the carnival and fair circuit. We'd work the shows, you as a ride operator and mechanic and me working the ticket booths or game joints! Then I got pregnant, and you said we can't go on the road with a baby, so you made me get an abortion, and then you left me, without saying a word!"

"Wait a minute Lilly. It's true I told you we can't go on the road with a baby, but I never told you to get the abortion. You did that on your own, without even talking to me about it!"

Whatever bravado Lillian had mustered for her long-awaited day in court with this horrible man vanished immediately, as if the wind in her sails suddenly left her dead on the water. He was right, she remembered correctly, he never told her to get the abortion, he never even suggested it. She took it upon herself, so driven to be with him. So all these 27 years she blamed him, when she should have taken responsibility and forgiven herself.

"Lilly, I was shocked when you told me what you'd done. If you'd had the baby we could have worked something out, I don't know what, but something. I was making good money, you'd soon get your nursing degree...."

"With a baby?"

"Oh sure, you could have done it, you're tough."

That was true, she knew single nurses who managed it.

"I just knew," Matthew looked at her, "we couldn't travel with a baby. Nobody does on the show circuit. And," he shrugged, "I just wasn't ready to get off the road."

"But...you ditched me," she choked up. "I went to the Fairgrounds—I ran all the way from downtown—the day we were supposed to leave together, and you were gone. Not even a good-bye note. Nothing!"

"I know Lilly, I'm sorry," Matthew shook his head. "I didn't know how to handle it, and it was cowardly of me. But it was the abortion that did it. I wasn't expecting that from you, it scared me. To me it's like killing a child, our child. And then...well, I thought you did it because you didn't want someone like me as the fa...." Matthew choked.

Time stopped for Lillian. This isn't the way it was supposed to happen. This was something else again.

Matthew cleared his throat and continued. "It made me wonder if all the time you were with me, you were slumming, or trying to be something you weren't. So I was confused, but especially insulted...."

"*Insulted*?"

"You thought I was white trash, didn't you? You thought that all us carnies are white trash."

Lillian was slapped. Is *that* what she did? *Did* she consider him white trash? *Was* she slumming?

"I..." she began, but couldn't speak.

"Why don't you sit down?" Matthew said softly.

Oh this man. He always knows just where I'm at, every moment, and just how to reach me. Well, I may as well relax and enjoy it, like I used to. It's been such a long time. What's done was done. Lillian pulled the chair up closer to the bed and sat. "So," she took a breath, deciding to move ahead, "what have you been doing all these years?"

"Well I finally got my own kiddie coaster," he grinned proudly.

"You did? Congratulations! Is it the Miler or the Herschell?"

"Miler. Those Herschells are good rides, but they take too long to set up, even with three men. Besides, Miler's got higher capacity, and I can give the kids two circuits in the time the Herschell does just one. Only takes two men to set up, plus it takes less space, the show owners like that."

Lillian and Matthew could have been back in Seattle 22 years ago, sitting in one of the waterfront bars, sipping beer while he told her his dream, a dream she'd wanted to be a part of.

"So," Lillian asked, "are you in town with a show? The fair isn't on yet."

"No, not a show," he said. "You know the Codding Town Mall? Well, they got hit pretty hard when that new downtown mall..."

"Santa Rosa Plaza."

"Yeah, when that opened, all brand new. So Codding Town decided to open a kiddieland to draw customers. Just 8 kiddie rides, a train ride, carousel. They offered me a year's contract for my coaster. They'll take a lower cut than the shows do, I can make good money. I was setting up today when I..."

"I saw the report, Matthew. Next time hire a qualified electrician."

"Yeah, 220 volts is brutal." He sighed. "Anyway," he reached out for Lillian's hand, "I never thought I'd say it, but I'm tired of traveling. What if the new kiddieland fails, I'll have to go back out on the road. I don't want to. Am I going to have to sell my roller coaster and get a real job?"

Lilly was speechless, staring at Matthew's lean, tanned hand, the strong, sinewy fingers.

She couldn't put her hand in his. She wanted to, but she couldn't, because it would mean.... Oh God, is this really happening? Didn't you promise this to me just a week after the accident, a little over a month ago? I didn't believe it then. I wanted love, needed love, and this happens.

"Lilly, I'd like to see you," Matthew kept his hand out. "Are you still living in that little seaside town you're from? What's the name?"

"La Sangre. Yes."

"La Sangre! Oh that's right, where Pete Freeman was killed!"

Lillian flinched. His death was still fresh, to her, Sal, Connie, Corey...all who knew the truth.

"I'm sorry, Lilly," Matthew withdrew his hand slowly.

"Oh no, Matthew," Lillian said earnestly, "it's all right. I'll tell you about it, what the media didn't know."

"Well, why don't you invite me over for dinner and you can tell me then. Remember how you used to cook for me, on that single hot plate in my room in Seattle?"

Lillian got up from the chair and went to the window, she wasn't ready for Matthew to see her tears, she wasn't ready for any of this, period. From the window she could see the tall revolving sign that landmarked "Codding Town." It was so close; close to the hospital, close to La Sangre. It was all coming together. 48 years old and suddenly her world was coming together.

She grabbed a tissue from the box on the table to dab her eyes, then turned around to Matthew and placed her hands on her hips. "Matthew Elijah Grant, I have just one thing to say to you." She paused, asking God for the right words.

"Yes?" he kept his eyes on her, his mischievous smile in place.

"If you're going to keep your boots under my bed, you miserable sonofabitch..."

"Watch what you say about my mother."

"...all right, you Jack Kerouac Wannabe..."

"Better."

"...you're going to marry me, we'll live in my house in La Sangre, you'll smoke outside..."

"I quit years ago."

"...and we'll go to church together every Sunday morning!"

Lillian watched as Matthew, with no hesitation, scooted to the far edge of the mattress and patted the empty space beside him.

"Okay," he grinned at her.

SEVEN

SANTA ROSA DISPATCH
August 22, 1984

WEDDING ANNOUNCED

Lillian Elisabeth Walker and Matthew Elijah Grant will take their wedding vows on Saturday, September 29, at noon in the La Sangre Christian Church in La Sangre. Reception to follow.

Miss Walker was raised and still lives in La Sangre, and Mr. Grant is from Topeka, Kansas. Miss Walker is a nurse at Santa Rosa General Hospital, and Mr. Grant has had a career in the traveling carnival industry and now helps operate the new Codding Kids Town. They met at the Seattle World's Fair in 1962.

Corey parked his new green Ford Ranger pickup truck—a graduation present from his grandmother Grace —in the student parking lot of Monterey Bible College. He grabbed his duffel bag and went to the outdoor table with a sign "Welcome Freshmen!"

"Corey...uh, Freeman," he said to the pretty coed at the table. He was still getting used to his new name, having dropped Satori. He told his parents that there was so much trash news and speculation about what had happened in La Sangre that he didn't want to have to deal with it everywhere he went, especially at college. Sal and Connie understood and co-signed the petition to the State of California for his name change. If Sal was hurt by it, he kept it hidden. Connie just gave a resigned shrug. She didn't want to have to think about it one way or the other. They were doing enough cleanup as it was, with both their family and the town.

"Hello Corey, I'm Elsa," the welcome girl told him. "Your dormitory is just over there. You can go on in and they'll give you your room number and key." She looked at her watch. "The cafeteria is just opening up for lunch. The dorm front desk will give you your meal card."

"Okay," Corey nodded and smiled at her. "Thank you!"

"Welcome to Monterey Bible College!" she smiled back.

So far so good. He was going to like this, he thought as he walked toward the dorm. The campus was beautiful, just as he remembered when he and his parents visited it on their way back from Pete's funeral. It was on a bluff overlooking the southern end of the Monterey Bay, within the sound of the ocean, just like...

Just like La Sangre.

He found his room, with a duffel bag sitting on the bed on the left. His new roommate had evidently already claimed his half. Corey dumped his bag on the right bed and looked around the symmetrical room with a combo closet/dresser, bed, and desk on each side. He looked out the window, it had a view of Monterey Bay and the ocean. Great. He went downstairs.

The cafeteria was large, bright, and mostly empty, he could have sat anywhere. There was a cute girl sitting by herself, long blonde hair pulled back from her face, clean white skin, no makeup. She was wearing a white blouse, buttoned up to her neck, a light blue scarf around it. Nice figure from what he could see. Corey hesitated, then told himself that she was probably just as nervous as he was. This was college. This was what you do. He approached her.

"Do you mind if I join you?" he asked, not without a small tremor in his voice.

"Well, it must be God's will!" she said brightly.

"Oh...sure," Corey responded with some discomfort. He thought he left all that silly La Sangre talk behind him, now that he was out in the real world. He placed his tray across from her, sat down, bowed his head in quick silent prayer, and looked up at her. "Hi, I'm Corey."

"Hi Corey," she gave a perfect-teeth smile, "I'm Tammy. So, what are your gifts?"

Corey looked at her. "I'm sorry?"

"Your *gifts*. Your ministry. How are you going to serve the Lord?"

"Well, I haven't thought too much about it..."

"Are you going to be Pastor?"

"I don't know. My father is."

"Oh really!" her eyes widened. "Where?"

Corey was expecting this, and was prepared for it. The La Sangre tragedy was just two months old, and already the trash newspapers like *The National Enquirer* were printing photos of Peter Freeman alongside photos of La Sangre, especially the church, with headlines like "SUPER BOWL WINNER MURDERED BY RELIGIOUS CULT?" Sal's La Sangre businesses—the gas station, antique store, saloon, grocery store, and general store—could barely keep up. Like the Gold Rush towns it replicated, La Sangre became a boom town. But to Sal it was blood money that he caused. He used only enough of the revenue to cover the overhead for the businesses and the church, and put the rest into charities.

"Sacramento," Corey answered the girl, Tammy, still uncomfortable with lying. Maybe he'll get used to it. But after a few minutes of forced conversation, with Corey describing his

Dad's church and small congregation, the girl seemed to lose interest. Corey managed to take a few bites while talking, but she had finished and was looking for a way to leave. He knew he wasn't any good at this, maybe he should be more aggressive.

"Say, uh," he ventured, "would you like to drive up into Santa Cruz some time? I haven't really gotten to know the area yet."

The girl placed her paper napkin on her tray. "Well," she looked away, "you know the Apostle Paul says that it's better to be single than to marry, because you're more free to be a better minister and to do God's work."

Corey looked at her, but her eyes were elsewhere. How did she leap to marriage? He thought his was a casual invitation. Maybe it was too much, too soon. "I just thought," he found himself checking his words, "we might go to the Boardwalk, ride some rides."

"The Santa Cruz Beach Boardwalk?" She gave him a look of disapproval and shook her head. "That's a very carnal place!"

"Carnal?" Corey mulled over the word. Maybe because of the beach? People wearing swim suits, girls in bikinis?

"Well," the girl smiled too brightly, perfect teeth and all, as she stood up and grabbed her tray in obvious escape. "See ya!"

She rushed off, leaving Corey with his cube

"So...." This was a lot for Corey to take in. "So you're just here for the curriculum."

"Mostly. But I'm also seeing this as a retreat, some real time alone with God. I know He exists, that's not a problem, but I'm just looking for myself I guess. This is a great way to do it, really do some Bible study, serious prayer time. I got enough money, I don't have to work for a while." Chuck studied Corey, whose brain was obviously full. As usual, Chuck knew he had gone overboard. "Hey kid, I'm sorry, I talk too much, always have. It's my Spanish blood. Maybe you should room with some young guy. I don't want to mess you up."

But Corey liked it. He stood up.

"Thanks Chuck. No, I want you for a roommate. I want to get smart."

"Well, all right," Chuck looked doubtful. "But I try to keep my big mouth shut. And you just say 'Callate, amigo intimo!' Okay?"

"No hay problema. Me gusta lo que dices." Corey looked out the window that faced the ocean. "But hey, I'm taking off for a while."

"Aren't you going to unpack?"

Corey regarded his duffel bag on the bed. Somehow he liked how it sat there, unopened, he could just pick it up and leave any time he wanted. A comforting sense of impermanence. He can start making decisions in his new his own decisions. He also knew Chuck

steak, mashed potatoes, and peas, wondering what he had done wrong, and how much he didn't know about this so-called real world.

But maybe this isn't the real world. Maybe he hasn't really left La Sangre after all.

When he returned to his room his new roommate was putting his clothes in the closet. They introduced themselves, Chuck de Angeles was his name—"like Los Angeles, but small D-E," he explained—and continued unpacking. He looked older, like maybe thirty, thick dark hair, a heavy four-hour beard, small firm body, like a younger, more compact version of his father...of Sal Satori. He was wearing jeans and a Bob Dylan tee-shirt, with hairy arms and chest hair poking up past the collar. They broke the ice easily, Corey sticking to and even embellishing his Sacramento story. Chuck was from San Diego, and already had an engineering degree. He noticed Corey studying him.

"I look a little old to you?" Chuck asked him.

Corey shrugged. "I don't know, I guess so. What are you..." Corey faltered.

"What's a 32-year-old guy doing at a Bible College?"

Corey shrugged again.

"I'm going to find out, and this was the only place I thought I could do it."

"Find out what?"

Chuck started putting his socks and underwear in the closet dresser. "Find out if God does have some kind of plan for me."

"Oh, that."

"Yeah, that." He stopped unpacking and sat down on his bed, facing Corey. "Hey man, I don't want to be a bad influence on you, but I'm hip to the Christian scene here. Maybe it's this way at every Bible college, I don't know."

"The Christian scene? Oh I know about that. Like I told you I'm from a small church. I just thought people would be smarter in college." Corey told him about the encounter with the girl in the cafeteria.

""What are your gifts?"" Chuck smirked. "In secular colleges they ask 'What's your major?' If you tell a girl 'pre-med,' you've got her. As far as her saying the Boardwalk is a *carnal place*. Well get used to it Bud. She's majoring in what most of the girls at a Bible College major in, husband-hunting." He considered it. "Yeah, the same as secular colleges. Either way it's what's your major, or gift, and how much are you going to make. Materialism and security cross all faith boundaries."

Corey was dumbfounded. "So what's the difference then, between this place and a secular college?"

"None that I've seen, socially, but I'm choosing this place for the curriculum. I'm not

interested in any girls here, I'm too old f
and they're too young and dumb for me
told this girl that your father is the pa
small church, right?"

Corey nodded.

"Now, had you said a big churc
congregation of at least a thousand,
have impressed her. See, that's the ɪ
a good-looking boy whose father pa
church, you both get your degrees ɪ
married, she keeps up her piano pla
two of you work at your Dad's ch
Dad's church—starting out as yoɪ
and working your way up to Ass
and when the old man kicks the k

Corey was taken aback.

"Oh, I'm sorry kid...Corey."
sidered his attitude. "Just be cɛ
Like I say, this place is no differ
lar college, or the corporate wo
know."

"How's that?"

"I was trying to be what I
mal. I got an engineering d
married my college girlfrieɪ
away in LA as a structura
good money from the start.
rate rules and played the ga
I realized I hated my job anɪ
We got divorced, no kids, ɪ

would be around for more talk. This was all new and good. He extended his hand to him.

"Where are you going?" Chuck asked him, shaking his hand.

"That carnal place. The Boardwalk. Maybe I'll ride the roller coaster. Uh, you want to go?"

"Naw, been there done that. But I'll pray for you Bud, at that so-called carnal place," Chuck grinned. "Oh, you know there's the orientation dinner at 6 PM, and some kind of shenanigan after that, prayer and worship probably, listening to a couple of the deans talk about how wonderful it is to be here." Chuck stopped himself. "There I go again. Mi boca grande. Are you sure you don't want another roommate, someone a little more..." he stopped himself again and winced.

"A little more 'Christian?' Yeah Chuck, I'm sure. Thanks."

"It's my job." Chuck paused thoughtfully. "Even though I'm still not very good at it."

As Corey walked to the parking lot, he wondered what Chuck meant by his last remark, but he tossed it and drove his new truck to Santa Cruz.

Dr. Ralph Owen, Pastor Sal Satori, and Doyle Seeno met in Sal's home office. Ralph and Sal had agreed that Sal's office would be more comfortable for Doyle than Ralph's, more Christian and less psycho. On that day it was also more private, with Connie out of the house for her first visit with a gynecologist in Santa Rosa, as well as shopping for maternity clothes.

The three men sat in cushioned swivel chairs in a triangle, the shrink with his professional comforting manner, the preacher man unfamiliar with all this, and Doyle wishing he was back at the gas station.

"Doyle," Dr. Owen began in a voice that was caring without being patronizing, warm without being too fuzzy, "are you uncomfortable doing this?"

Doyle kept his gaze on a sentimental yet comforting painting on the wall, Jesus praying in the Garden of Gethsemane, a gift from the congregation on Sal's last birthday. He shook his head.

"Have you ever been to a doctor before?" Ralph asked him. This was his standard operating procedure with new, frightened patients. His questions and reactions hardly ever varied; he had explained the routine to Sal.

With Doyle still looking away, Ralph made brief eye contact with Sal, which per their agreement meant Sal should speak up.

"Doyle," Sal said, doing his best to match Dr. Owen's tone, "remember about two years ago, you injured your hand while you were changing a customer's tire?"

Doyle's eyes remained on the painting. He nodded.

"Do you remember what we did?"

Doyle nodded again. Sal waited for a response, looked back at Dr. Owen, who nodded for Sal to proceed.

"Remember, Nurse Walker looked at it, and she thought..."

"She thought it might be broken," Doyle spoke unexpectedly, in almost a little boy's voice. Sal looked at Ralph. We got him, Ralph nodded to Sal. Go ahead.

"You've always liked Lil...Nurse Walker, haven't you Doyle?"

Doyle nodded, still lost in the painting, but listening. "She is always nice to me."

"And do you remember what she suggested?"

Doyle nodded again. "She iced it, and said we ought to have a doctor look at it, to see if any of the bones in my hand were broken. So you..." Doyle finally turned to Sal, "you drove me in to Santa Rosa, we went to the doctor. You stayed with me the whole time."

Sal gave Doyle a warm look, and the first hint of love for this man he'd known for ten years but merely took for granted, and in fact shamelessly used as a tool, magically appeared. Doyle sensed it, became uncomfortable, and looked back at Jesus in the garden, finding warmth in the golden glow around Jesus' face.

"Doyle," Sal continued, "what did the doctor do?"

"He took x-rays."

"And what did the x-rays show?"

"Bruised, not broken."

Sal looked at Ralph, who winked at him, their sign that Ralph would take over.

"Doyle," Dr. Owens began cautiously, "very often our feelings, our emotions, our sense of well-being, can be bruised, and possibly even broken, just like your hand. And psychiatrists, like myself, are trained to help the patient examine himself, decide if anything emotional is bruised or broken, and he can help the patient recover."

Doyle turned from the wall print to Dr. Owen and nodded.

"Doyle, do you want to tell me about the dream you've been having, the dream you told the Pastor about?"

Doyle turned back to the painting, wishing he could jump into it and just stay there. Oh Jesus, he pleaded, help me!

EIGHT

Corey spent the afternoon at the Santa Cruz Beach Boardwalk. He did a couple of rides, and then bought a pair of swim trunks and towel at the gift shop so he could try out the small waves of the bay.

The waves were gentler here on the north shore of the Monterey Bay than the ferocious waves at Jenner Beach, just south of La Sangre, where he usually went body surfing in a wet suit. But the water here was warm, very pleasant, and the beach was certainly more crowded than the more secluded and less accessible Jenner Beach.

He sat on the sand for a while, watching the girls in bikinis. They looked very nice, happy, not at all self conscious, not at all "carnal," whatever that was. After a while he realized he should get back to Monterey. ("Prayer and worship," Chuck had said, "listening to a couple of the deans talk about how wonderful it is to be here.")

Instead Corey got dressed and walked onto the Santa Cruz Wharf. He found a small restaurant and checked the menu in the window. It was affordable enough, it wasn't crowded, so he went in, and yet another pretty girl—are they all pretty in Santa Cruz?—showed him to a counter that faced the water. He pulled a menu from the counter rack and gave his order to the (pretty) waitress.

"May I sit here?" a low, rich voice asked.

Corey turned to his right. "Uh...sure!"

She was a vision; tall, toned, tan, perfect. Long dark brown hair cascading over her bare shoulders. She gave him a closed-mouth smile with full lips. No lipstick, in fact, little or no makeup on this bronze beauty in a tank top and shorts, expensive sunglasses perched over her head. Older, probably in her thirties, maybe older, there was no apparent age to her.

There were at least three empty stools to his left and to her right; she could have chosen any of them. Yes, this was better, much better than that silly girl in the cafeteria, even better than all the Santa Cruz girls he'd seen so far.

The waitress set Corey's Coke in front of him and turned to the lady, the beautiful lady.

"Coffee please," she said to the waitress, and picked up a menu from the holder. She barely glanced at it. "What did you order?" she asked Corey.

"Uh...a bacon cheeseburger."

"That comes with fries, doesn't it?"

"Yeah."

"Do you like onion rings?"

"Oh, I like them fine. I just went with the fries."

"Good, then I'll order onion rings. I see you have a Coke, but they make good milkshakes here. What flavor do you like?"

"Uh...chocolate I guess."

"All right." She placed the menu back in the holder and waited until the waitress returned with her coffee. "I'll have onion rings and a chocolate shake."

The waitress nodded and left, and Corey suddenly realized he was staring at this goddess sitting next to him, at her cleavage. He blushed. She gave him an easy smile, not seeming to mind. "You have to order food to sit here, especially this time of day. They don't want tourists using this place for free sunset-watching " She appraised the empty stools. "Funny, there aren't usually so many stools available, especially with it getting toward sunset. I was afraid I'd have to wait. I'm glad I didn't have to."

"Uh, yeah, me too."

"You too what?"

"I'm glad you sat next to me...I mean...."

She smiled again, this time showing strong white teeth. Corey liked it, he liked it all, her dark brown eyes, lashes. Yeah, better than the girl in the cafeteria. Way better. "I'm sorry," Corey caught himself.

"Sorry for what?"

"Well, it's just...it's not polite to stare."

"That's okay, I don't mind. But let's watch the sun for a bit, it's just starting to head down. There are clouds on the horizon. We'll have a nice sunset." She pulled her shades down over her eyes.

They were quiet until the waitress brought their food. The beautiful lady moved her plate of onion rings and the chocolate shake so that they were between the two of them. "I don't want them," she told Corey. "You're a growing... young man, aren't you?"

Corey nodded, not knowing what he was doing.

"Then eat, drink. Just keep them here between us, so my space at the counter is properly paid for. I'm good with just coffee." She reached into her purse, still on her lap. "Do you smoke?"

Corey shook his head, wondering if he gave her the wrong answer.

"Well then, neither do I." She placed her purse on the stool to her right. "Now," she turned to him, "eat." She poured some cream into her coffee and sipped.

Her presence made Corey suddenly very hungry, and he began to devour his food without saying grace, while she watched him.

He followed her gold BMW twenty miles north on Highway 1 to Waddell Beach, where a small, wood-shingled house sat next to the road on the beach side. He parked his pickup next to her car and followed her inside.

The small living room was full of colors, colors Corey had never seen before. The furnishings were all different colors, and like the modernist paintings on the wall, the colors neither matched nor complemented each other.

"I'll be right back," Maria said, going into her bedroom on the left, leaving the door open. He heard a toilet flush, water running. She came back out. "Do you need the bathroom? It's back there."

Corey shook his head. He was enjoying this unfamiliar excitement. Somehow the disparity of colors was working on him.

"Wild," was all Corey could manage.

"What is?"

"How we met," Corey grinned. "Being here."

She smiled back. "Let's go out to the deck. Would you like a beer?"

"I uh...sure!"

She grabbed two bottles from the refrigerator, opened them, and led the way out to the deck. The sun was long down, but the sky was still a screaming orange, the ocean's roar complementing it. They stood against the railing. She raised her bottle to his and they clinked.

The beer tickled Corey's taste buds, his throat, but went down nicely on top of the bacon cheeseburger. He was full but still not satisfied. The newness of the beer thrust him into an exciting unknown. "I don't believe this," Corey half mumbled.

"Nice, isn't it?"

"How could you...I mean, this house out here all alone on Highway 1. The CCC..."

"California Coastal Commission? Oh, you know about them? Sure, they'd love to get rid of this shack, they consider it an eyesore, but it's been grandfathered in, my family's owned it for decades. We can't sell it to anyone but the State of California, who'll probably tear it down, or turn it into something for their own purposes, a maintenance shack for Highway 1 probably."

Maria looked out to sea, a confident smile on her face. "How about a swim?" she turned to Corey. "You didn't eat too much to swim, did you?"

"No, I'm good. I'll have to grab my trunks from the car."

"You don't need them. It's getting dark. Nobody can see us from the road. It's all right."

She was undressed before he was. He fumbled with his clothes, unable to take his eyes off her. Plus he was a little embarrassed, having a.... well, he saw legs all his life and liked them, so he always thought he was a leg man. But maybe he's a boob man. But it didn't matter with her; she wasn't the sum of different parts, she was total, complete, everything.

Maria turned from him before she could see his excitement, and ran down the steps and across the narrow beach to the water. He watched her, then finished undressing, and ran down to join her in the shallow surf.

"Ready?" she asked.

Corey nodded, grateful that she kept her eyes on his, didn't look down at his embarrassment. She took his hand and they ran together towards a particularly large wave, and dove through it, a little painful for Corey in his condition. They emerged and treaded water, looking westward in a wave-watch, the sky's orange getting brighter each second. Corey looked at her; he could look at her forever. He didn't even know her name and he was almost afraid to ask, as if identifying her would wake him from this dream.

"What's your name?" he finally asked.

"Maria."

"I like it."

"What, my name?"

"No," Corey grinned like a kid at Christmas. "I mean, yes, I like your name, but…"

"Then, what else do you like, Corey?"

"But…how did you know my name?"

"You told me at the restaurant, don't you remember?"

He did? No, he didn't remember.

"So Corey, what is it you like?"

"I like how..."

"Yes?"

"How...your boobs float above the water."

She gave a soft chuckle. "It's more than that though, isn't it? Not just my breasts, but the water itself, the sky—look the moon's already out—the sound, even the headlights of the cars on Highway 1...don't worry, they can't see us. Isn't it *all* wonderful?"

"Wonderful," Corey managed, shallow-breathed.

"Wonderful," she repeated softly.

Like a powerful, warm, loving shark, her hand reached out under the water and without searching or fumbling, took hold of him.

"Oh God!" Corey groaned at the orange sky.

NINE

Dr. Owen knocked on Sal's door around eight in the evening.

"Come on in Ralph," Sal greeted him. "We'll go up to my office. Babe," Sal turned to Connie in the kitchen, "we won't be long."

"Would you like something Doctor," she asked. "Coffee?"

"No, thank you Connie. And please, call me Ralph."

"Ralph," she smiled and nodded.

"Well," Sal said as he closed the door to his office. "I think Doyle understands, somewhat, that psychiatry isn't the devil's work. But that's not to say he's atypical, because his prejudice is certainly the norm in evangelical churches."

Ralph sat down. "I understand that. Going below the surface into one's self is like heading off to war, and a lot of people use religion to avoid looking at themselves. By the way," he nodded to Sal, "you did pretty well with Doyle."

"Well, thanks for prompting me. So, what about his dream?"

"I believe he was sodomized," Ralph shook his head. "Horrible thing to do to a child. One of the occupational hazards of being a shrink is finding out what happened to helpless children, seeing their pain...and wanting to hang the perpetrator by the balls."

"Helpless children," Sal furrowed his forehead. "Doyle has said to me 'My daddy beat the hell out of me,' like it was something he was proud of, a badge of courage."

"The good old Texas beating, it's called," Ralph agreed. "Many young men do consider it a rite of passage to manhood; better that than admit they were brutalized by someone bigger and stronger than themselves, someone whose love they craved. They usually pass it onto their own sons. After all, if it made them tough, it will make their boys tough."

Sal nodded, grateful he'd never given into the occasional temptation to hit Corey. "So, where do you go from here?"

"Where do *we* go from here, partner. I'm not sure yet. I want to get some facts first. I went to the library this morning and looked up the town of McCarthy, Texas, where this apparently happened to Doyle. McCarthy is unincorporated, and has a population of about 100..."

Like La Sangre, Sal thought.

"...and it's in Borden County. I'm going to call the County and request crime information.

We know from Doyle's telling of the dream that he was five years old, so I can at least figure out the year the horrible crime happened. I'll see what details I can get, it'll help me get a timeline. What happened at what age, and consider the effects."

"When should we meet with him again?" Sal asked.

"Let's give him some respite. That was quite a breakthrough he had; it takes a lot out of someone to go through that in therapy. We'll wait and let him muse. He might even initiate something, more likely with you."

"And what should I do in that case?"

"Just listen to him, but try not to ask any questions. Leave that to me. But you could ask him if he'd like the three of us to talk again. Okay?"

Sal nodded. "Thanks."

Ralph stood up and extended his hand. "God works in mysterious ways...so I'm told."

Sal shook his hand, looking at him expectantly.

"Oh no Sal," Ralph shook his head, "I'm a died-in-the-wool atheist. My job is healing people, not saving their souls. I'll leave that to you."

"Well, I'm enjoying working with you."

Ralph slapped Sal on the shoulder. "But as we Marines said during World War II, 'We're buddies okay, but don't try to convert me.'"

"You also said that there were no atheists in the foxholes."

"No," Ralph responded pointedly. "I never said that."

The next morning Dr. and Mrs. Owen were sitting on their front porch sipping their coffee. They were wearing their windbreakers; it was cool but pleasant.

"So," Ralph said, "how did your foray into Bible study go?"

"Oh," Anne said vaguely, "all right I guess."

"You came in late. It must have been... interesting?"

Anne found herself getting annoyed. During their almost-thirty year marriage, he never once divulged any information about his patients, which she knew was a golden rule for shrinks. But now she wanted something of her own. Maybe instead of just giving him information for his book on La Sangre, she'll write one of her own.

"What's the matter?" Ralph asked her.

She couldn't say "nothing" to her husband. He was a good psychiatrist, he could read her— and everyone's—tone, nuance, choice of words, emphasis, de-emphasis. He could spot lying in a second. But dammit, she was going to allow herself her *own* privileged information.

"That's okay, you don't have to." Ralph was right along with her, as always.

Dammit, she said again to herself. I *will* tell him something. Give him a teaser. She turned to him, covering her coffee mug with her hand to keep the heat in. "I will tell you one thing, Ralph. You know Ruby, the one who lives in that obnoxious pink and green cottage that the neighbors yap about?"

"Ruby," he pondered. "Obese, with bright red-dyed hair?"

"Yes. When the Bible study ended last night, she asked me to walk with her to the cliff, she had something to tell me."

"What did she...oh, sorry, against the rules?"

Against the *new* rules, Anne thought triumphantly. "I'll tell you just one thing, Ralph. She told me that she knows what the secret of La Sangre is."

Ralph turned to her. "But she didn't actually tell you what it was, right?"

"Right." His astuteness stopped surprising her years ago, back in college in fact.

"*The Secret Of La Sangre*," Ralph mused. "You know, that might be a good title for a book. Kind of corny, like a romance novel, but it might be good."

You know, Anne considered to herself, it just might be.

"Jooo-leee, I'm ho-ome!" Nathan gave his endearingly lousy Ricky Ricardo impersonation as he came in.

"Kitchen!" Julie called back.

He put his briefcase in his office and went into the kitchen, where she was bent over at the open refrigerator. He slapped her in the ass, she turned around with a casserole dish and give him a kiss, handing the dish to him. "Put that in the oven, will you? 375 degrees."

"Yes, dear."

"Never mind the smart remarks, because right now I'm jealous. I think you have a new girlfriend. Guess who called for you just a half-hour ago?"

Nathan furrowed his forehead then looked at her, eyebrows raised. "Darryl Hannah?"

"Not even close. Remember Ruby, one of the people you tried to interview in La Sangre?"

"Ruby? Oh yeah, fat with Lucille Ball hair."

"You've got 'I Love Lucy' on the brain."

"Oh you know that show always makes me frisky," he put his arms around her ever-expanding waist.

Julie nodded toward the note pad next to the wall phone. "Well, not until after nine o'clock, because that's when she wants you to call her."

Nathan looked at the phone number. It was the La Sangre exchange all right. "Did she say anything? She sure stonewalled me, like everyone else in that crazy town."

"Well, she said just one thing. She wanted me

to tell you she knows the secret of La Sangre."

"*The Secret Of La Sangre*," Nathan repeated softly. "It's kind of girly, but it beats *Death Of A Football Player*."

"Yeah," Julie agreed. "It does sound like the romance novels all the desk nurses at the hospital read. You know, while they're ignoring the call board."

But Nathan didn't respond. This interview with Ruby, this could be it.

This really could be it.

"Hello?" answered a shrill yet cautious voice.

"Ruby? It's Nathan Steer. My wife said you asked me to call you."

Silence.

"Hello? Ruby, are you there?"

"Oh yeah, sorry, I was looking around, making sure no one can hear me. I'm at the new phone booth in front of the gas station. The Pastor had it installed after the accident, when he told us we all have to get our own private lines. We used to have to go through Mary for an outside line. I don't have the money to get my own line."

"You mean no more going through Mary The Snoop Operator?" Oops, that was bad. He needs to ingratiate himself to the town, not set himself apart by making fun of it.

But Ruby enthusiastically agreed with him.

"Mary The Snoop she is, you should hear the gossip she spreads, and the lies. But none of us really minded, it was fun. You know, sometimes we'd plant false gossip while she secretly—or so she thought—listened in to our calls, just to watch how she'd spread it. One time I told one of the ladies over the phone that I was pregnant, and didn't know who the father was!" Ruby began to cackle. "You should have seen Mary, running all over La Sangre with her mouth flapping! 'We really have to pray for Ruby, because she...'" and Ruby's cackle got even louder. Certainly, Nathan thought, the entire town could hear that, even from the phone booth.

Nathan waited for her to come down. "Ruby, my wife told me that you know the secret of La Sangre."

"I certainly do," she answered proudly.

Nathan waited. "Well, can you tell me about it?"

"Not without a hundred dollars, Mr. Newspaper Man."

"A hundred dollars," Nathan repeated without surprise or argument.

"And..." she paused.

"Yes, and what?"

"Well, I'll tell you all about the secret, while you buy me dinner at The Tides Restaurant in Bodega Bay. But you'll have to pick me up, I don't have a car."

She was making a date, Nathan knew. Julie wasn't wrong. "That's fine."

"*And* you're buying me a lobster!"

Nathan felt like laughing with joy. This phone conversation alone will certainly go into his book, secret or no secret. "All right, but just a lobster tail. I don't want to be showered with lobster juice."

"They give you a bib!"

"Lobster *tail*," Nathan said with kind authority. He had to push back on something to maintain his position.

"Well, okay," she gave in. "But I'm getting a steak with it. Steak *and* lobster tail. And a shrimp cocktail to start."

"Deal."

"And chocolate mousse for dessert!"

"Chocolate mousse, check. I might even throw in a bottle of wine."

"Wine? I'm a *Christian*!"

Nathan and his wife made tremendous love right after the call, and it was one of their best times.

"You were thinking about Ruby, weren't you sweetie?" she said afterward, her head resting on his board-flat, hairless chest.

"You betcha baby."

Julie and Lillian agreed to meet at a bench

next to the hospital parking lot when their shifts ended.

"This is the smoking place, isn't it?" Lillian asked Julie as they sat down.

Julie nodded. "As I said, I need to talk to you, but I couldn't do this in a restaurant."

"Sounds heavy."

"It is. Oh, there's no problem between us Lillian, that's all fine, great in fact."

"I'm glad to have a friend," Lillian smiled.

"Me too." Julie waited a few seconds. "Well, I guess this is where we'd light a conversational cigarette, if we were smokers." She took a deep breath. "Lillian, you were friends with Jessie Malana, is that right?"

"Well, no," Lillian pursed her lips. It was still an unpleasant subject, probably always would be. "I can't say we were friends, even though after her living there for nine months, we certainly had the opportunity. Neither of us pursued a conversation, and I never dealt with her as a nurse, she must have gone into town for any medical matters."

Julie nodded. "I saw her once in the ER, for something minor. She gave her address as La Sangre, and after the accident I put it together."

"She was hard to miss."

"I know, she knew what she had and how to use it."

Lillian nodded. "Even so, she always kept to

herself, even though she did attend church and the women's Bible studies."

"So, she was a believer?"

"Not that I could see. Matthew would say that's between her and God. She wasn't at all candid, not even during the women's groups, which could get quite intimate. Oh, she'd read along in the Bible like the rest of us, she'd ask questions, but she never opened up to anyone about her personal life, that I know of. It's interesting that the one time I wanted to talk to her, and actually needed to talk to her, was that Saturday morning just before Peter Freeman came into town. I was in one of my rages, my 'I-Hate-Men' mood that would happen during my period, where I'd rant and rave to God and myself, blaming Matthew for, so I thought, making me have an abortion, and then dumping me."

"So you vented to Jessie?"

"Not really," Lillian chuckled, "though I wanted to. I approached her in my mood to trash men."

"Oh, like on 'The Sally Jessy Raphael Show!'"

Lillian laughed out loud. "Exactly! Except..." she stopped laughing. "Except in Jessie's case... it obviously ran too deep, very serious."

Julie took a deep breath. "Which brings me to what I wanted to talk about, what Nathan thinks may be 'the secret of La Sangre.' You know Ruby, she lives in that awful colored cottage?"

"Ruby," Lillian closed her eyes. "Don't we all?"

"Well, she told Nathan she uncovered the so-called secret."

"Julie, maybe you shouldn't tell me."

"No, Nathan wanted me to, he decided to pass the reporter's cap to me for this. He appreciates our friendship and you're somewhat involved with this, being the de facto leader of the town."

"I suppose I am."

"Ruby told Nathan—for a hundred dollar fee, mind you—that poor Jessie was a victim of incest. Her father started having sex with her when she was just 8 years old. She was living in La Sangre to hide from him."

Lillian gasped. "That's horrible! How *dare* Ruby say something like that, let alone selling it for a hundred dollars! How *can* she say something like that?"

"She claims that Jessie told her this, after the last women's Bible study before the accident."

Lillian was stunned, remembering. "Oh yes...I was at that meeting. It was Friday night of the Father's Day weekend, and when we broke up, Ruby and Jessie walked over to the cliff, to talk I guessed."

Julie nodded. "Ruby told Nathan—and he believes her, I believe it myself—that Jessie told

Ruby she finally had to get it out, she had to tell a Christian, someone who would pray for her—but she made Ruby swear she wouldn't tell anyone else until after she died."

"You mean not until after Jessie died? But she...."

"She died two days later, on Father's Day."

Lillian also remembered her brief exchange with Jessie the very next night, Saturday night, when she was trying to find someone who would help Peter escape from La Sangre. Jessie declined to help. "Jessie knew she was going to die," Lillian stated it as fact. "She wanted to die."

"It seems that way." Julie exhaled. "You know that Nathan and I witnessed her crash into the barrier, without a seat belt, and..." she couldn't finish.

Lillian sat quietly a few moments, gathering her recollections. "Jessie's behavior, her attitude, her coldness, her simmering anger...it doesn't surprise me that she was a child of incest. She overused her sex appeal, her waitress uniform was too tight, too short. I was certain it was a power trip over the men in town, especially the Pastor." Lillian paused. "It shocks me but I can't say it surprises me. But what," she shook her head helplessly, "what do we *do* with this? Jessie is dead. Okay, Ruby made some money off it, and that doesn't surprise me either, but what does this have to do with any 'secret' of La

Sangre? I've lived there most of my life, and I don't know what this has to do with the town, idiosyncratic as it is."

"Well, Nathan is building a case that this poor damaged girl came into La Sangre looking for help. Maybe Dr. Owen and Jessie thought a quiet environment by the sea would help her, but apparently it didn't. And Nathan is pursuing that La Sangre in fact hurt Jessie with its religious fanaticism. But wouldn't Dr. Owen have known that about the town? If he thought it would hurt her he wouldn't have sent her there, even with the rent-free cottage."

"Yes," Lillian began to put it together, "I can see all the connections that Nathan is making, but...." She frowned. "I don't know, Julie, this sounds kind of...dangerous somehow."

"I know Lillian," Julie nodded, "I agree. I said as much to Nathan. I asked him if he does this book, what if Jessie has some long-lost relative around? There could be real trouble, legal and otherwise."

Corey stayed at Maria's beach home for two days. He didn't need anything, she had an unused toothbrush, he let his beard grow, and they were naked most of the time anyway, so there was no reason to interrupt two glorious days of sex, swimming, sex again, and sometimes eating.

On the morning of the second day, Maria

announced she had some work to do, so she set up her easel out on the deck, and began to paint, in the nude ("It opens me up for the creative flow," she explained), while Corey sunned himself and watched.

"Are you painting another like the ones you have up?"

"No," she smiled mischievously. "I'm painting *you!*"

"Oh," Corey became self-conscious. "Do you want me posed...another way?"

"Oh no, you can move. I'm painting your spirit."

Corey had indeed found his spirit, his manhood, and as he watched her paint, he followed her light beige body up from the feet, her strong smooth calves and thighs, soft rounded stomach, wonderful firm breasts, her neck...it was one long continuous ribbon that went upward from her feet to her face...oh that face. She wasn't the sum of those parts, she was whole, one entity, a meandering flow of beauty, all of which he had touched and kissed and couldn't wait to do so again. He watched as she took pleasure in her painting, stepping back to study, frown and critique, then joyously discovering her next color and applying it. He knew she was painting the real him, the man she had created with her love.

He fell asleep, naked in the sun.

His father, Sal, was standing naked at the cliff in La Sangre. Corey was standing on the deck of their home. He was a little boy, he didn't know how old, but his head was no higher than the railing. He watched as his father took a decisive step closer to the cliff. "NO DADDY, NO!" Corey cried.

Corey jolted awake.

Maria, standing at the easel, was starring at him. "No Daddy no?" she questioned him, her eyes alighting, her volume rising, turning shrill. 'NO DADDY NO!"

Corey was groggy. "Huh?"

"WHAT GIVES *YOU* THE RIGHT TO SAY 'NO DADDY NO!'"

A grayness engulfed her, as if a large smoke-glassed dome was lowered over her entire body, encapsulating her, trapping her. Corey stared, at the grayness, the angry eyes. "What? Maria? I guess I was...."

"DREAMING, I KNOW! BUT WHAT I WANT TO KNOW IS, WHAT GIVES *YOU* THE RIGHT TO SAY 'NO DADDY NO!'" She glared at him, ready to pounce; clearly, he was suddenly the enemy.

Corey was afraid. He didn't know how to act, what to say, what to think, didn't understand the question, and wondered who was standing there, hating him so.

She suddenly bubbled with enthusiasm.

"Oh, Corey, don't pay any attention to me!" The gray covering was instantly gone, her eyes back to their earthy brown. "I'm sorry, I didn't mean to wake you, but I'm just sooo excited! This may be the best spirit painting I've ever done!"

"Oh...sure...." The gray dome, the angry eyes, was probably part of his dream. "Uh...can I look?"

"Just one more dab...there!" Satisfied, she stepped back from the easel. "Okay, you can look!"

The painting would haunt Corey for the rest of his life. It was indeed like those on her walls, and like them, it was twisted, contorted, angry, evil. The pallet of colors weren't complementing each other, they were....

"They're...colliding," Corey said in wonder, in fear.

"I know!" Maria smiled proudly. "Isn't it beautiful? Okay, I'm done. Now I'll sign it for you."

The signature wasn't completed because Corey suddenly grabbed her and pulled her down and took her on the deck, while she laughed. This time it was faster and more furious than ever before, wanton, frustrating and angry.

All Corey told the girl at the front desk of the Monterey Bible College dormitory was that he was checking out, period. He'd missed the orientation, the campus tour, the indoctrination sessions, and he didn't care. He'd gotten "indoctrinated" all right, he laughed raucously to himself as he drove north on Highway 1, back to Waddell Beach. "Oh Maria, you're the girl for me-uh!" he sang off-key to the road, to the ocean, to his new life.

He pulled up to her home, his home now, he was sure, but was surprised to see a second vehicle parked next to Maria's BMW, a black, full-sized Dodge pickup. He managed to squeeze his Ford Ranger behind her BMW, assuming whoever owned the truck would be leaving soon. It was probably some repairman. He got out and walked back to make sure his rear bumper was clear of Highway 1. That was when he noticed the mailbox bearing the name MALANA.

"Malana?" Corey said out loud. Was that her last name? Maria Malana? He realized Maria never told him her last name. What had it mattered? She didn't know his last name either, and had never asked him.

But Malana. As in "Jessie" Malana?

Was it a common name? Or just a coincidence?

Corey looked at the house, at the front door.

He knew something was waiting for him inside. During the drive up he was ready for Sex Round 21. He'd actually counted while they were together, telling her he wanted to reach 20, which they did, easily. Corey was certain it was a record for anyone.

But he discerned this time it would be something else, waiting inside.

Not a repairman.

Something very wrong.

TEN

The Incredible Hulk answered the door before Corey lifted his fist to knock. This guy was huge, his frame completely blocking the door, his chest pushing out from a "GOLD'S GYM – NO PAIN, NO GAIN!" tee-shirt, a size too small, arms bulging.

"Hey Baby, he's here!" he half-shouted not taking his eyes off Corey's.

"I *told* you not to call me that!" she ordered from within. "Well, let him in, stop showing off!"

He stepped aside, just enough to let Corey in. "You're in for it buddy," he said to him.

"Knock it off Brutus!" Maria told him.

"I told you not to call me that!" he shot back and slammed the door.

"Bruno, Brutus, what's the difference?"

He opened his mouth in response but thought better of it.

Marla was sitting in her favorite chair, purple leather. "Sit down Corey," she ordered him, pointing to the green love seat.

Corey hesitated, looking at Bruno.

"Oh, don't mind him," she waved Bruno off. "He's just here to protect me, in case you try to get violent. Like you did that one time when I was painting on the deck and you...oh never mind."

Bruno flinched.

Corey was frozen. What was this? He'd heard about shakedowns, about something called the badger game. Was this it?

"Sit down," Maria repeated with annoyance, "you're not going to get hurt. Not if you tell the truth."

"Just don't try anything, pretty boy," Bruno warned, "or I'll throw you right out onto Highway 1 and claim it was an accident. Or I'll take you into the ocean and hold you under like..."

"Shutup Brutus!" Maria raised her voice. He stiffened up, but once again decided not to retort. "Go to the kitchen and get the boy a beer. Or would you rather have a Coke, like at the restaurant on the wharf?"

Corey didn't answer. He couldn't. The restaurant on the wharf? That felt like a lifetime ago. He sat down, and looked around. Yes, this was the right house, the same living room that had been cozy, warm, wild, crazy. Now it was cold and scary. All he could do was look slack-jawed at Maria. What *was* this?

"Yes my dear," she changed her position in her chair, adjusted a throw pillow at her side.

Her long beautiful body that Corey had feasted on was completely covered by by a long-sleeved, high-neck jumpsuit. "Yes Corey, I have some explaining to do. First of all, did you see the mailbox out front?"

Corey nodded.

"I had it covered before you arrived here, which probably wasn't necessary. You were so ready with your permanent erection you probably wouldn't have noticed it."

Bruno slammed the bottle of beer on the kitchen counter.

"Yeah," she half-yelled to him, "as if I'd ever give *you* a tumble, you Lou Ferrigno Wannabe!"

He glared at her and came out of the kitchen with the dripping bottle.

"Anyway," she turned back to Corey, "it was all very well designed, don't you think? Bruno watched your truck in the parking lot at that silly Bible college...."

"A lot of cute chicks there," Bruno said as he handed the wet bottle of beer to Corey.

"Like any of them would give *you* a tumble!" Maria shot back. "They'd laugh at you. Now just go stand by the door and do whatever it is I'm paying you to do." She turned back to Corey. "So Corey, Brutus the Dud-Stud...."

"Bruno!"

"*Bruno* followed you to the Boardwalk and then called me. I drove down and he pointed you out walking onto the wharf and, well lover boy, the rest, as they say, is history." She gave him a pointed look. "Definitely. History."

It hurt. Bad. "How...how did you..." Corey stammered.

"How did I know *who* you were, and *where* you were? Since Jessie's death I've had a little spy in La Sangre; of course I'm not going to reveal her name, but she kept me in the loop about what was going on in that sick little town of yours. She reported that you were coming down for some orientation at that ridiculous Bible college, and that's when I decided the time had come. After two months, the time has come."

"Time...for what?" Corey managed to ask. What was this woman talking about?

"Time for revenge, my dear." Maria reached for a pack of cigarettes, offering them to Corey first. "Oh, how stupid of me, the preacher's kid doesn't smoke. Well that's all right, I think you've found your drug of choice, thanks to me."

Corey shook his head, trying to understand. "Jessie is your sister? Your younger sister?"

Maria lit up and took a deep drag. "Yes, we're 13 years apart. She was only 24 when she died, but she looked ten years older, didn't she? I'm only 38, and I look like I'm in my late forties, I know that. It affects us that way. It makes us old before our time, it makes us hard, it makes us wise. It makes us understand what sex is, and how to use it."

"What does?"

"Incest, you stupid God-Squadder! Jessie was my younger sister, but she was also my daughter! MY DAUGHTER! DO YOU GET IT NOW?"

It was ugly. Insane. It made horrid sense. ("What gives *you* the right to say 'No Daddy no!'")

Maria's lifelong refrain hung in the small house for a moment, then settled like rancid dust over everything, and everyone. Bruno lowered his eyes, while Corey was in a horror movie that was really happening.

Maria leaned back in her chair and took a drag, satisfied with Corey's stupor. "Yes, you Christians really are stupid, aren't you? You believe these types of things only happen to bad people, to sinners, because if you're a good Christian, then nothing like that could ever happen, isn't that right? Just pray and act stupid and you'll go straight to heaven. But people like me and my sister, my daughter, won't get into heaven, will we? We're marked for life, and you Christians patronize us. 'Oh, if you'd just get right with God,' they tell us. And just where is this so-called 'loving God' who conveniently looks the other way while my father fucks me at 13, and then fucks my daughter, my sister, when she's eight? EIGHT YEARS OLD! WHERE

WAS YOUR FUCKING GOD THEN? WAS HE LAUGHING AT IT? WAS HE GETTING OFF ON IT?"

Then silence.

The only sound was the Highway 1 traffic.

I should be out there, Corey yearned, driving along with the rest of them, just living life like they are. Going to work, going to school...I never should have left Monterey Bible College. ("I'll pray for you Bud, at that so-called carnal place," Chuck said. He wasn't kidding.)

Maria turned to Bruno, who had dutifully positioned himself at the front door, proud that his frame completely covered it. "Okay Bruno," Maria suddenly and effortlessly lowered her volume and softened her tone, "I think you can leave, I don't need you. I'm all right."

Bruno slowly shook his head in disagreement.

"Oh okay, maybe not," she reconsidered, "you never can tell." She turned back to Corey, who hadn't taken a sip from the beer in his hand. Just its smell made him want to throw up, through he'd drunk plenty of them over the last two days. They had even spilled beer on each other during the lovemaking.

"I just want to ask you one question, Corey. And you'd better not lie to me."

Corey stared at her.

"Corey, did you fuck my daughter? My sister? Did you fuck Jessie?"

"No!" he blurted out. He'd never even thought about that. He'd noticed Jessie, sure, everyone did. But she scared him. He couldn't forget how she had verbally attacked Pete in the saloon, and all Pete did was walk in the door and take a seat. He and Pete were trying to have a conversation, but Jessie kept interrupting, like she was angry and jealous of how Corey enthused and idolized Pete. "No," he said again, definitely.

"Then why did she try to run you over with her car? Sex made her go crazy, she couldn't do sex! Neither can I, except for when it serves a purpose, like I did with you."

Corey jolted. That's all it was. Sex with him was her revenge.

"I asked you a question!" Maria said. "Why did my sister try to run you over?"

"I...I don't know," Corey responded weakly.

Maria was suddenly quiet, reflective. She can change so quickly; Corey remembered the painting incident on the deck. Plus there were moments, especially during the sex...she'd suddenly go into a daze, bleak. He just thought it was part of the sex, and he went along, not knowing.

"Yes, I believe you, Corey," she finally said softly, with a wan smile. "And I should have known. I could tell you were a virgin." She suddenly looked around the room as if someone was there besides Corey and Bruno. "But, if you didn't fuck her, then who did?"

"I...I don't know, Maria! I barely knew Jessie. I never saw anyone go into her home, never saw her with any man. She hardly ever left town, probably just into Santa Rosa. There was nobody, not even a girlfriend. She talked to the cook in the Saloon, but only because they worked together." Corey could see Jessie now, behind the counter. "She always had the radio on to the country station, and she'd sing along, real lonely like, but then she'd change it back to the Christian station when my father...the Pastor came in."

Maria studied him, and she too saw her daughter, her little sister, listening to the radio and rocking back and forth. She started doing that when she was eight years old. Maria lowered her eyes.

"I believe you, Corey," she sighed in resignation. "I do. You're a good kid. You haven't yet learned how to lie. Oh, except when you changed your name from Corey Satori to Corey Freeman. You chose the name of the football player who saved your life. Why did you do that? Sentiment? Or you just don't want to be associated with that town, you being the Pastor's Kid."

She leaned back in the chair. "Well anyway," she sighed again, "I'm going to find out who fucked my sister. I'm staying in touch with my La Sangre contact, and when I find out who did it, I'll cut that motherfucker's balls off." She turned to Bruno. "Well, I think we can let this kid go, Bruno. I think he's had enough, for a lifetime in fact."

"Yeah," Bruno echoed stupidly, "I think he's had enough too."

"I didn't ask for your opinion, Brutus. You're a bodyguard, nothing more. Oh, you have a great body I guess, but you'll have better luck with it at the gay beach than with me, so don't try to score points with me. Corey, you can go now, back to your Bible college. But let me leave you with one thought."

Corey looked at her. She was softening up, and he began to see the Maria he had been with for the best two days of his life, soft, warm, loving. How they laughed, how they looked into each other's eyes. Maybe it was still possible, now that she knew he wasn't guilty of anything, maybe now they could re-connect, go back to what they had before. His attraction to her was still powerful, even after all this.

But that was all a lie, wasn't it? This part, what's happening now, is the truth.

"Corey, I'm certainly an atheist, but I can sometimes see why you people believe. I myself was impressed when my La Sangre contact told me you were going to Monterey Bible College, near where I live. I mean, how likely is that? There were so many other places you could have gone after high school, for college or work. Not that I wouldn't have still gone after you, I would have had you followed anywhere and brought you down. But you came right to me! It's those kind of things that make you believe, right? Well, if there is a God, He must be playing on my team right now, don't you think?"

Corey's momentary foolish hope turned to sickness. He hadn't tasted the beer, but the smell was burning his lungs.

"You don't look good, Corey. But let me give you one more thought. You know those two wonderful days you and I spent here, just yesterday and the day before. Weren't they wonderful?"

Corey stared at her.

"Weren't they?" she insisted.

He nodded dumbly.

"Well boy, you'll never have it that good again. Oh you'll search for it, but you'll never have it that good again." She kept her eye on him to make sure he'd heard her, then turned to Bruno and nodded. He dutifully opened the front door, signaling Corey's exit.

Shell shocked, Corey managed to stand up walk out the door. One foot in front of the other. Bruno slammed it behind him.

Outside in the sunlight he saw the cars on Highway 1 going north and south, not knowing or caring what had just happened in this obscure roadside house; to them it was same old beach shack that has been sitting there for over fifty years. They just drove by and never knew who lived there. Only Corey knew, and nobody would ever believe him.

He got to his pickup and rested his right hand the side of the bed. He realized he was still carrying the slimy untasted bottle of beer in his left. He dropped the bottle on the asphalt and it shattered. With two free hands, he grabbed hold of the side, steadying himself. Then he leaned over and vomited into the pristine bed of the Ford Ranger pickup his Grandma, Pete's mother, had given him for his high school graduation.

ELEVEN

THE SECRET OF LA SANGRE
by Anne P. Owen

CHAPTER 1

La Sangre is like a little jewel, an emerald, sitting on the coast of Northern California. People stop and look at its quaint stores and cottages and lovely ocean view. But like any jewel, La Sangre is flawed. Some people see those flaws, some don't. Most people just drive through it on Highway 1, but don't see the town as it really is.

When my husband and I bought our cute little cottage in La Sangre ten years ago, little did we realize the heartache, the heartbreak, the happiness, the sadness, the longing and the yearning, of the citizens of La Sangre. My husband, a famous psychiatrist, told me that La Sangre is like a litmus paper, which tests the strength and character, or lack of, any person that comes in contact with the town. But I myself see La Sangre as a red Rorschach ink blot, that people see in it what they want to see.

Anne leaned back in the kitchen chair, pleased and surprised. This sounded just like all the books she'd read, the autobiographies of the stars, like the one Doris Day did. She told us things about her life that nobody knew. So, my book will be geared to women mostly. It could even be serialized in *Redbook* or *Good Housekeeping*.

Now my husband's book will be totally different, of course, more for the trade and the serious reading public. So there will be no conflict of interest there, I know about these things. In fact, Ralph and I could even do the husband-and-wife TV guest thing, promoting our books. I mean, if Jim and Tammy Faye Bakker can do things like that in the name of God and make big money, why aren't we entitled to that? What makes *them* so superior? Yes indeed. I'd sure like to ask those Bible ladies that question: what makes Jim and Tammy so superior? Oh, they'd die, they'd just die!

She stood up from the table, ready to take her writer's break. She stretched and wondered about movie rights.

There was only one place Corey could go for some kind of answer, something to get him back on solid ground. He couldn't remember driving from Waddell Beach to Monterey, but he did, driven by the need to talk to someone who knew what all this meant.

"Chuck?" the girl at the dormitory front desk repeated. She was young but looked like an old librarian, with her hair in a bun and cats-eye glasses, far from the pretty girl who had smiled at him when he checked in. "So, does this Chuck have last name?"

Corey ransacked. He was sure Chuck had given his last name. "Oh yeah, 'Los Angeles.'"

"Oh, he must have a smoggy brain," said the girl in a snotty attempt at humor. Corey suddenly wondered if he was in the right dorm, or even on the right campus. What was sunny and bright when he arrived here was now, two days later, dark and humorless. She flipped through a card file. "No Los Angeles here."

"Oh no," Corey remembered, "it's *De* Angeles."

She flipped a few cards. "Well, that's not here either. What room were you assigned to?"

"532."

She looked in a separate file. "Corey Freeman," she read. "Room 532. You were the only one assigned to 532. The dorm wasn't full up, a lot of the new students don't come for the indoctrination. They'll be here in September. And you said you checked the room?" The girl was making no attempt to hide her annoyance.

"Just now," Corey nodded, "when I picked up my bag. There's no one there, no clothes, his bed wasn't slept in."

The girl frowned at Corey, and looked at

another boy approaching the desk. "May I help you?"

"So, how can I find him?" Corey was desperate.

She looked back at Corey. "You can ask the Registrar's Office. There's a campus phone right over there." She scribbled the number on a pad, tore it off and thrust it at Corey and said again "May I help you?" to the other young man.

The Registrar Secretary crisply advised Corey that there was no such name as Chuck or Charles De Angeles registered for the Fall Semester, nor for the Student Indoctrination Program.

Corey wasn't surprised. His world was now off center.

August 24, 1984

Dr. Ralph Owen
General Delivery
La Sangre, CA 94923

Dear Dr. Owen,

In response to your request for information about the sexual assault on Doyle Seeno, Case # 7566602, I can tell you that he was sexually assaulted by a Mr. Wesley Wallace on May 15, 1950, at the perpetrator's house in McCarthy, Texas. The medical examination of the boy showed anal abrasions and lacerations, indicative of sodomy. The boy also had bruises elsewhere on his body, suggestive of further physical abuse. While he was immediately given proper medical attention, I do not see that he was ever given any psychiatric treatment, at least not as long as he was a minor living in McCarthy, this was before Child Protective Services. Doyle left McCarthy right after high school graduation.

Wallace was convicted by a judge of felony assault on a minor and sentenced to 20 years in Federal Prison at La Tuna, Texas. Two weeks after his incarceration he was murdered by inmates who undoubtedly knew of his crime.

Doyle Seeno's parents are both deceased, and he has no siblings. He does have one surviving aunt, his mother's sister, living in Fort Worth under her married name of Victoria Banks. I can't give you her contact information, but she shouldn't be difficult for you to find.

I hope this information on such a horrible crime is helpful, and I pray your treatment of him will lead to a healing.

Sincerely,

Ben Williams
Borden County Sheriff Department

"Grandma?"

"Corey? Oh, I'm so glad. Your mother called me earlier today, you haven't returned home yet and she's worried!"

"Yeah, yeah...I...I went to Monterey Bible College...I...I can't go there again Grandma..."

Grace almost responded with "But you've got a full scholarship!" but stopped herself. They'll have time to talk, now's not the time. "Corey, where are you now?"

"Fresno. I left Monterey yesterday...didn't know where I was going, I spent the night in my truck, I've just been driving. Thank you again for the truck Grandma...."

"Of course Corey. If you're in Fresno now, why don't you..."

"Can I come see you? I don't know what I'm going to do."

"Yes, yes, I was just going to say that. Are you all right to drive?"

"Yeah, I'm just..." he choked.

"That's okay sweetie. We can talk when you get here. Just drive south on the 99 to Bakersfield, take the Ming Avenue exit. It'll take about an hour and a half this time of night. Don't drive too fast. Do you remember how to get here?"

"I think so."

"Well, just call me if you get lost. I'll leave the light on at the front gate, and the gate will be open. I'll call your parents..."

"NO!"

"Corey, I *have* to, they're worried!"

"I turn eighteen next week, I can do what I want!"

"But you're seventeen now, and they have to know, Corey."

Corey was silent for a moment. "Okay, but just talk to my mother, not Sal."

Grace took a breath. "He'll have to know, but okay, I'll make sure I just talk to her. I'll tell her you're going to stay here for a few days. In fact, you'll sleep in your father's old room, all right?"

Corey closed his eyes. Finally, something good. "Okay Grandma, thanks. I'll see you soon."

"Drive carefully Corey. I love you."

"I love you Grandma."

Oh Mabel, I couldn't make the women's Bible Study because both kids have a cold. I know Mary, we prayed for them. Thank you. So tell me, did that Mrs. Owen show up? Oh yes, she did, and oh, you should have been there. Really? What happened? Well she sure asked a lot of questions. Really? Like what? Well, she asked if drinking is a sin. She didn't! Yes she did. We all see her and her husband drinking wine on their porch. If I was a Catholic I'd cross myself when I see that. So what did you say? Oh, I didn't say anything, Opal answered her. Really? What did Opal tell her? You should have heard her, Opal said, 'drinkers and smokers do *not* get into heaven!' Oh my! And what did Mrs. Owen say to that? Well, she just kind of smiled, but we'll have to see if she and her husband have their wine again tonight. Well anyway, we need to pray to release the demons that are inside her, you know, not just the alcohol but being the wife of a psychiatrist and all! Do you think we should pray for her husband too? I mean he *is* a psychiatrist. Oh, I don't know Mary, I guess we should, so that he'll realize the error of his ways and give up that demonic profession...if you want to *call* it a profession. Amen to that!

"Nathan, I've been thinking about it," Julie said at breakfast, "and after talking with Lillian the other day, I don't know."

"You don't know what?"

Nathan and Julie cherished every third weekend, when her rotating schedule allowed her both Saturday and Sunday off. They always ate their breakfast in the patio, under the arbor that Nathan had kind-of built.

Julie took a sip of her coffee. Nathan always made better coffee than she did. "I don't know if...well, if your book is the right thing to do."

"What do you mean..." Nathan began with a mouth full of scrambled eggs.

"Chew and swallow."

"You sound like my mother."

"Well, maybe I'm practicing for it."

Nathan's eyes went wide.

"*No*, I got my period as usual. I just don't know if writing the book is such a good idea."

"And your reasoning?"

Julie set her mug down and considered their life. This was so nice, sitting here, a beautiful morning in Sonoma County. They could sit around the house and do nothing, maybe some yardwork or housework, or maybe go for a drive, visit one of the wineries. They could do anything they wanted, life was all theirs. They were fortunate, they didn't have the kind of childhood that.... "Nathan, what happened to Jessie, what happens to children all over the world, is horrible! Although I've never seen it myself, I know that children have been brought into the ER that are victims of rape and incest. I'm afraid you'll be opening a Pandora's Box that you may not be able to deal with."

"Yeah, I know," Nathan set his fork down. "To tell you the truth, after crazy Ruby told me that about Jessie—and I do believe her, although her motive is lousy..."

"A hundred dollars in exchange for a damaged child's life."

"Yeah." He took a sip of his coffee. "What I think I'll do is pursue it as far as I can, and then turn it over to someone for academic input. Like maybe that psychiatrist, Dr. Owen, in La Sangre.

After all, he treated Jessie in Redding, though it apparently didn't do her much good, and now he lives permanently in La Sangre."

"Well, what do you mean by 'pursue?'"

"I'm going to try to uncover any relatives or close friends of Jessie, and see what happens. I already went to the Santa Rosa Library and went through the Redding white pages."

"Find anything?"

"Only that Malana is a very common Spanish name. Lots of them. Plus variations, Malani with an 'I,' Malany with a 'Y,' Malane with an 'E.'" The root is "mal." Do you know what that means in Spanish?"

Julie shrugged. "I only took Latin in high school, you know that, preparing for the medical field. Now do you mean 'mal' as in 'malignant?'"

"Right. It means bad. Evil. Anyway Jules, I'm going to search for 'Malana' up in the Sacramento Hall of Records. See, Mexican farm workers with that name wouldn't have any state records or social security numbers, so that would weed them out. I'll just see how far I can go with it, and what I come up with."

"Good luck."

Corey woke up in his father's old bed, the best sleep he'd had since he and Pete spent the night in the room over the gas station, over two months ago.

He looked around the room. His grandmother had gotten him situated when he'd arrived after eleven. "It hasn't changed since his college days," Grace had told him.

"But it doesn't look very...I don't know, high school." Corey said. "I was expecting trophies, framed news clippings, stuff like that."

Grace shook her head. "He changed it while in college. He was in a fraternity at UCLA, but he didn't much like all the partying, so he came here whenever he could. Spent a lot of weekends when it wasn't football season. That's when he bought all the prints." She pointed out the large print of Charles Russell's "Wagon Boss" and Van Gogh's painting of olive trees bathing in a golden sun. But the one that Corey liked best was James Fraser's "End Of The Trail," with the Indian hunched over his horse, down but not out.

Corey craned his neck and body around so he could look at "End Of The Trail" hanging over the headboard. He knew that painting, it was a landmark sign for the Journey's End Trailer Park on the Old Redwood Highway in Santa Rosa. Corey loved it as a kid, and now knew how that Indian felt; it must have been how Pete felt when they met. Down maybe, but not out.

There was a quiet knock on the door. "Corey," Grace said softly. "Are you awake?"

"Sure Grandma, come on in!"

She opened the door just enough to put her head in. "Did you sleep okay?"

"I haven't slept this well since the night that..."

Grace closed her eyes briefly. "I know." She pointed to the bathroom. "There's plenty of clean towels in there, help yourself."

"Pete...my dad had his own bathroom?"

Grace nodded. "With four sisters we decided that a young man should have his own bathroom. The girls had two bathrooms between them and there were still fights. When you're finished, come on out to the kitchen and I'll make you some breakfast."

"Okay. Grandma?"

"Yes?"

"I'm glad to be here."

Grace smiled and gently closed the door.

August 29, 1984

Dear Ruby,

I just got your letter today and wanted to respond right away. As you probably noticed, I have changed my fake name again on the return address. You told me that Nurse Walker no longer runs the General Store since she took a full time job at Santa Rosa Hospital, and I don't trust those La Sangre gossips not to try to look inside or hold it up to the light to see what this letter contains. I can't help the Santa Cruz postmark, but if any of them ask who the letter is from, just tell them it's a Christian pen-pal from Santa Cruz.

I got rid of Corey after a couple days, and got all the information out of him I could, which was only that Corey isn't the one who had sex with Jessie. But I still scared him and I'm not sorry, because he's the Pastor's son and who knows what crazy ideas his father must have put into my sister's head, like if you have sex outside of marriage you're going to burn in hell. And as you Christians say, the sins of the fathers are visited upon their sons, so Corey had something coming to him.

You told me that you saw that newspaper guy snooping around again, asking questions, and that he and his wife have visited Nurse Walker a couple times. Maybe you could knock on her door when he's visiting, and tell Nurse Walker you need some kind of medical help, and in that way find out what that guy is doing. Or give him some false information to throw him off the track about my own personal investigation.

You also said that the pastor and Dr. Owen have been visiting each other. What can that be about? I thought you Christians hate

GARY KYRIAZI

psychiatrists. Anyway, keep an eye on those two.

Attached is another check for $100. I appreciate anything you can tell me.

And remember, burn this letter after you read it, and I'm burning yours too. No you don't have to burn the check, ha ha.

Maria

Corey and his Grandmother had breakfast by the pool. Corey thought he'd stepped into a movie about rich people...rich and famous people no less.

"This is nice here, Grandma," Corey told her as he finished his pancakes and sausage. "I'm happy to be here."

Grace had decided to wait until Corey finished eating before she began to lecture. She knew the boy was going through hell. So was she, for that matter.

"You know Corey," she leaned back in the patio chair, holding the china cup and saucer, "I never considered myself a particularly religious woman. Oh, I was raised that way, but my husband was a non-believer—though he never really used the word atheist—and he had a large prosperous business to run. But the way things have happened, losing my husband and son ten days apart, I hated God, or at least

♦ 144 ♦

whatever I thought God was. But now, with what has happened since then, just within the last two months, finding out that Peter had a child...." She smiled into her coffee cup. "You told me that Peter knew you were his son, is that right?"

Corey nodded. "Only that morning, just minutes before he died. My fa...Sal told him that my mother got pregnant by some guy in high school, and Pete knew it had to be him. I wish I could have seen what Pete looked like when he found out."

Grace continued to look into her coffee. She would liked to have seen that too. "Anyway, these past few days, all of a sudden things seem to be working out in a new way, the way they're supposed to. Oh, I'm still grieving, but somehow..." She looked around the pool area and the tennis court...it had all seemed so worthless and empty two months ago. Still she was more fortunate than most women going through this. The lawyers advised she'll never have to worry about money for her or her children, the house and acreage are paid off, Lawrence Freeman Produce is in great shape, continuing to grow, not overextended. Then of course there was her husband's million-dollar life insurance policy. All four daughters live in the area, they have four grandchildren among them, all girls. And now she has a grandson, a new chapter in her life. She was already adjusting to it.

"Corey," she looked at him peacefully, "something's going on in both our lives, something new. I don't know exactly what, but I know one thing: you and I are going to figure out together what you're going to do."

Corey wiped his mouth with his napkin. "All I know Grandma, is that I don't want to go to college. Or not until I know what I want to study. Sal said that I could at least do the first two years of college and get all the general ed requirements out of the way, and then figure out my major. But right now I don't think college is for me."

"Well Corey, it may not be, it isn't for everyone. Your father hated school, except for football. Worse, he knew that Lawrence Freeman Produce was waiting for him, like some big monster that might devour him. Once football was over after he won the Super Bowl, well, he was wealthy and didn't have to work. He loved his home on the beach in San Francisco, he was talking about building a second home in the redwoods and he could have afforded it. But in your case..."

"I'm not rich. And Grandma, I won't depend on you for money."

"Well, there is your father's estate you know, you're his only child."

"No, I appreciate that. But I want to support myself."

"I know you do. And you know, whatever your father's feelings were against Lawrence Freeman Produce, it may be a good fit for you. Your grandfather loved his work, and obviously did well at it." She didn't add that the stress of the job killed him at age 57. But Corey was third generation, some traits skip a generation.

Corey looked at the swimming pool, rippling from the morning breeze; maybe he'll take a dip later. It was all so nice here: his Dad's room, the breakfast, and his grandmother's love and concern.

He suddenly remembered last night. After calling Grandma from the truck stop, he'd settled down some, knowing he had a place to go. In the parking lot he saw a truck whose trailer read "Lawrence Freeman Produce – America's Finest." It felt like a road sign for him. He went into the cafe and sat one stool away from a middle-aged, burly man with a cowboy hat who looked like he could be the driver. Corey took a chance.

"You drive for Lawrence Freeman Produce?"

"Well I transport for them, but no way I'd work for them. They run too tight a ship for me. I'm independent."

Independent. He liked the sound of it. Now, poolside with his Grandmother, owner of Lawrence Freeman Produce, Corey knew what he wanted. Whether it was God or not, it didn't matter. This was Corey Freeman's decision, not anyone else's.

"I'm going to be an independent trucker," he announced to his grandmother, and to himself.

SEPTEMBER - DECEMBER, 1984

TWELVE

"With the power vested in me, and in the name of the Father, the Son, and the Holy Ghost, I now pronounce you Mr. and Mrs. Matthew Grant. You may kiss the bride."

"Oh!" Matthew raised his eyebrows at Lillian. "Can we rehearse that too?"

"Hey," Lillian slapped Matthew playfully on the arm. "We've already rehearsed that. Tomorrow during the ceremony is good enough."

"Well," Sal grinned, as long as you remember that it's always customary for the Pastor to kiss the bride."

"I won't forget," Lillian smiled back at Sal. "And *that* we can rehearse!" She gave him a peck on the lips. Matthew rolled his eyes.

Seated at the organ, Connie was happy not just for Matthew and Lillian, but for all of them, including Julie Steer, who was here for the rehearsal. She really didn't mind that Lillian chose Julie as Maid of Honor; their work at the hospital had made them close. Besides, Connie told herself, who wants to look at an obviously pregnant

Maid Of Honor? And somebody has to play the organ during the ceremony, even if playing always reminded her of a lonely young Connie-Cooty practicing the piano daily in Bakersfield.

But this was the strongest sense of family that Connie had experienced in her twelve years in La Sangre. Matthew was a long-needed shot in the arm for the town, his refreshing candor and borderline cocky personality able to disarm anyone. Surprisingly, or perhaps not so much given the change that had come over Sal, Matthew and Sal got along fine, not unlike Sal's unexpected friendship with Dr. Owen, who in fact was attending services regularly with Anne. Even if he was humoring his wife, it didn't matter, they were both joining in with the La Sangre people, as best they could.

"So Connie, will there be music at the reception?" Matthew asked her after he gave Lillian a simple kiss on the lips. "I want to dance with my bride." He grabbed Lillian in a dance hold and faked a few steps.

"Now Matthew, let's not spring too much on them at once," Connie chuckled, getting up from the organ "But whenever we do, promise that I'll get to dance with the groom. He," she lightly nodded at Sal, "never dances with me."

"Aw, give me time," Sal put his arm around Connie. "I never learned."

"I'll take care care of that, Sal," Lillian said.

"And don't worry Matthew, there is a jukebox at the Tides Restaurant, and it has 'Lady' by Kenny Rogers, just like you asked. I checked."

"So," Sal said to the four of them, "are we ready for tomorrow?"

"I think we are," Julie smiled. She was happy to be a part of it, and for a second even considered talking to Nathan about moving there.

So Blanche, did you go to the wedding? Oh yes, it was the right thing to do, of course. And wasn't that a lovely dress Nurse Walker was wearing, a long yellow gown with yellow carnations? Oh yes, but you notice that she didn't wear white? Well, she's almost fifty after all. So what do you think about her husband? Oh I don't know, he seems so...so coarse. Well, he travels—or *used* to travel—with a carnival, and you know how they are, with all the drinking and the drugs and the wild sex. Oh I know what you mean, when I take my kids to the county fair and I see all those godless roughnecks running those rides...and I'm *sure* those rides aren't safe. Oh they're not, and they're all doped up on who-knows-what when they put those rides together. I won't let my kids ride. Oh me either. Well anyway, do you think Nurse Walker's husband is saved? No. I asked him when I first met him, you know, just to be polite, how long have *you* been saved? And you know what his answer was? What? He said, well that's between the Lord and me, in a sarcastic tone. Really? The nerve! I know, but still we're just going to have to pray for him, won't we? Oh yes, we'll just have to pray for...what *is* his name anyway?

Corey and his grandmother made a verbal agreement. She would pay for trucking school, as well as a new sleeper truck out of Peter's estate, and Corey would pay it back with workable monthly payments. Furthermore, whenever he wasn't on the road, he would stay at her house, in his father's room. She would talk to LFP's shipping department and put her nephew into contract consideration. She'd vouch for his character and besides, a little nepotism never hurt anyone.

"I guess that's fine, Grace," Connie said tentatively over the phone when Grace outlined Corey's plan to her. "No, I *know* that's fine," Connie corrected herself. "I'm...just trying to get used to all this. I told my parents Corey is staying with you, and my mother is hoping she'll at least run into Corey. He probably won't call them."

"I understand all this honey. I raised five kids. Peter was a perfect child, but the girls...I've spent too much time wondering what I did wrong. And all I'm guilty of is one thing: being a mother to those girls. Their father didn't have time for discipline—something that Peter didn't need—so I was stuck with the dirty work. I was the mean one and their Dad, who was never around, was their hero."

"I thought Peter was their hero."

"Oh he was their protector all right, but they drove him crazy like sisters do. Anyway, as they became adults, when one of them didn't want to speak to me, you know, 'Don't call me, I'll call you,' I had to learn how to let go. That was hard."

"Tell me about it."

"Oh Connie, I know Corey's rejection must be awful. He just has to go through it, and you and I can just hold on together while he does. I do know he loves living in Peter's room, it's a way of getting to know him. He found Peter's book of poetry from high school."

Peter writing poetry in high school? Of course, Connie realized, it fit in with everything he told her their one night together. She wondered if he'd ever written a poem about her. Wouldn't that be something if Corey uncovered one of Peter's poems titled "Connie."

Connie sighed. "Thank you Grace. And..." she hesitated, "I can call you any time I like? I won't abuse it."

"I know you won't Connie, and yes, you can call me any time you like. As long as I can do the same. I need support too, you know."

"Of course Grace. Twenty-four seven."

In his search for a relative or some kind of associate of Jessie Malana, Nathan had to do a certain amount of subjective exclusion. There were Malanas all over the country, let alone the state. He had no choice but to just deal with California and judiciously concentrate on certain towns. He found the most Malanas in Bakersfield, which stood to reason because of the farming, but significantly Bakersfield was Peter Freeman's home; he was Jessie's victim, could there be a connection? Then again, Lillian said Jessie hadn't pointed her car at Peter, but at Corey. So Nathan marked Bakersfield as unlikely. Redding was more likely. It had only a couple Malanas, but it was where Jessie had been living for a few years and sought treatment with Dr. Owen.

Nathan went to a print shop and ordered a fake business card that read "Sam Diamond, Private Investigator," enjoying the contrivance and not caring if it was over the top. He then took a weekend trip to Redding and went to all the addresses he had with a story about being hired by the State of California regarding a Miss Jessie Malana, who recently died intestate. As he expected, every Malana he talked to was interested, some even claimed they were a relative but could offer no details on her, or else their stories were laughably fabricated. ("Oh yes, that poor dear. She was my cousin. She died of cancer, didn't she?") Even those who were up on the media frenzy couldn't contribute anything more than what they read in the supermarket checkout lines. "Yes, she was my cousin, and she *told* me she had an affair with Pete Freeman!"

So Redding was a bust, but before he pursued Bakersfield, one particular name that jumped out at him was a Maria Malana of Santa Cruz. It was the closest location to La Sangre at 140 miles, whereas Redding was 240 miles away. He should have done that first.

"I'm going to drive to Santa Cruz next weekend to check out a Maria Malana," Nathan told Julie. "Her address is Highway 1 at Waddell Beach, just north of town. You feel like going? We can get a beach motel in Santa Cruz, you can sunbathe and check out the studs while I sleuth."

Julie didn't even have to consider it. "No, remember I owe one of the nurses that weekend, both days, no way I can change it."

"Oh yeah. Well, I guess the following week..."

"No Nate, you go ahead, really. By the way, didn't any Malana in Redding ask why you didn't just write to them?"

"Yeah, one did. But it's better if I can see them in person, what they look like. Jessie Malana was a very fair woman, likely of Spanish descent, not Mexican. I can't ask that in a letter."

Nathan found the lone beach house at Waddell Beach, with a mail box marked "Malana." He knocked on the door, and an astonishingly beautiful woman with long dark hair answered.

"Excuse me," Nathan went into his well-practiced spiel, "my name is Sam Diamond, and I'm searching for any relative of Miss Jessie Malana, who died with property and without a will. I'm trying to locate any family she may have." He handed Maria his business card. She took it but didn't look at it, keeping her eye on Nathan. ("This newspaper man, Nathan Steer is his name, has been snooping around," Ruby had told her in a letter. "He actually invited me to dinner at the Tides Restaurant, thinking I might have some information on Jessie because I live in La Sangre. I had steak and lobster tail. It was real good. But he's skinny and ugly, and he got nothing out of me.")

Maria shook her head. "I'm sorry, I have no siblings, my parents are both dead, no aunts or uncles or cousins." She wanted to know how much Nathan knew without seeming interested, as she casually asked, "Who was this Jessica Malana?"

"*Jessie* Malana," Nathan politely corrected her. He didn't volunteer anything else. "Well, thank you. I'm sorry for disturbing you."

"Not at all. You're welcome," she said curtly and shut the door.

She went directly to the phone. "Bruno, you have to start keeping an eye on that newspaper guy I told you about, the one who writes for the *Santa Rosa Dispatch,* and did the AP wire piece. He was just here, asking if I knew Jessie.... No that's fine if you need to hire someone up there, do so, just don't gouge me.... No, not Nathan *Bull,* you idiot, Nathan *Steer.*"

"Yeah, Santa Cruz was a bust, along with Redding," Nathan told Matthew and Lillian while he and Julie were having dinner at Lillian's—the newlyweds' – home.

"So now you're going down to Bakersfield?" Lillian asked as she got up to clear the dishes. "No, sit," she ordered Julie who had stood up to help.

"Yeah, I guess so," Nathan exhaled. "But I'm thinking it will be another bust."

Matthew had been studying and listening to Nathan throughout dinner, saying little himself, trying to decide if he liked this guy. Lillian and Julie had become very good friends, so he was obliged to go along. "Lilly," he asked over his shoulder, "are you going to serve dessert now, or later?"

"A little later, I think. I'll make the coffee now. As our mothers used to say, 'Why don't we all go into the living room?' It's too cold for the front porch."

Matthew looked at Nathan. "First, how about us boys going into the den...*my* den," he teased Lillian, "for some gentleman talk?"

"Sure," Nathan said, "but I don't smoke cigars."

"I got something better."

Nathan raised his eyebrows.

"No, not that." Matthew didn't hide his annoyance at what he thought was Nathan's carny/druggie presumption. He went to the cupboard over the refrigerator and removed a bottle of Jack Daniels. "This," he said to Nathan, "is the secret of La Sangre." He grabbed two shot glasses. "Come on Nate, let's give the ladies a chance to talk about us."

Matthew led him into the den and closed the door. It was warm and comfortable, with dark wood paneling, chocolate brown carpet, an antique roll-top desk, and two comfortable brown leather chairs. A bookshelf was well stocked, there were a couple of framed carnival posters on the wall, a framed 8x10 photo of Matthew proudly at the hand brake of his kiddie coaster, alongside a portrait of Franklin Delano Roosevelt.

"Nice den," Nathan commented.

"Yeah, Lilly sacrificed her sewing room for it." Matthew noticed Nathan looking at the FDR portrait. "He's my hero," Matthew said.

"Why's that?" Nathan asked, his investigative reporter mode kicking in.

Matthew ignored the question. "Sit," he pointed to one of the chairs. He set the shot glasses on the desk and filled them, handing one to Nathan, and raising his own. "Here's to *The Secret Of La Sangre*...whatever it is."

They clinked and sipped. Nathan wasn't very much of a drinker, but this was good, smooth, and he nodded appreciatively.

"I'm curious Nate," Matthew settled himself in the other chair. "Do you know what your motive is in writing your book?"

Nathan was taken aback. "Well, to be honest..."

"To get published, right?"

Nathan shrugged. "It'll be a good start."

"Oh I agree. Lilly has been telling me I should write a book about my 35 years traveling as a carny. She teases me as a Jack Kerouac Wannabe."

"I read *On The Road*."

Matthew nodded. "I'd use that title if Kerouac hadn't already stolen it from me. But I have to ask myself, what would I be trying to say, besides titillating the reader with stories of the alleged wild life after the lights on the Ferris Wheel go out and the ride ops, barkers, and freaks kick back. What would I want the reader to understand, to learn from it?"

Nathan took a sip. "I guess I'll have to work on that myself." He decided to pursue another route. "Matt, I don't understand why you're living here, in La Sangre. I mean, I know this is where Lillian's from but..."

"But why is an obviously intelligent, independent man living in such an insular religious community?"

"Well...yeah."

"First off, who wouldn't want to live next to the ocean? But to answer your question, I do take a kind of perverse pleasure in being here. You know us carnies are considered the greatest sinners on earth, mainly because we don't *look* right and we don't *act* right, whatever 'right' is supposed to be. All right, we're no saints, but we know who we are. To answer your question, and perverse pleasure aside, do you think it's easy for me to keep my mouth shut in this town? Check Matthew 7, verses 21 through 23."

"I don't have a Bible."

"Get one, and read it like you would a Robert Ludlum novel. It'll take you places you never imagined." Matthew reached over to the desk and grabbed the Jack bottle. "There was a famous lady in the early 1900s, Emma Hendrickson, a very great lady. Jolly Trixy was her stage name. She was a 685-pound Coney Island 'freak.' Her show banner read 'She's so fat it takes seven men to hug her and a box car to lug her.' Some time around 1910 she said to a *New York Times* reporter, 'If the truth be told, we're all freaks together.'"

Nathan was stunned. "Wow. 'We're all freaks together,'" he repeated softly.

Matthew raised the Jack bottle. "Another shot? To Jolly Trixy?"

The whole town had been invited, but Doyle wasn't able to make himself go to Matthew and Lillian's wedding two weeks ago. He couldn't use the excuse that he had to tend to the gas station, as one of the La Sangre teenage boys would have happily covered for him for a couple of bucks. So Doyle made up some excuse that he had to go to Sacramento to pick up some parts, that everyone knew was a lie. He wasn't jealous, but he couldn't be happy for them, because he himself was so...unhappy, and lonely. Church wasn't enough. He was realizing that for the first time in his middle-age life.

He'd had three sessions with Dr. Owen, with the Pastor sitting by, and indeed the nightmares had slowed down some. But now Dr. Owen, with the Pastor's support, wanted Doyle to look at what those nightmares meant. "What do you remember when you were a child?" Dr. Owen would ask him, and Doyle would turn to the Pastor for help, but Sal would only nod in encouragement.

"I don't want to go back there, Pastor," Doyle told Sal one morning, catching him during Sal's regular walk through the town.

"You mean back to Dr. Owen?" Sal answered, surprised.

Doyle nodded.

"Can you tell me *why* you don't want to continue the therapy? It seems to be helping. You said the nightmares stopped."

"Well, not completely, they're just not as bad." Doyle looked away.

"Okay. But you know that any time you want to talk to Dr. Owen, or to me, or to both of us, you can."

Doyle kept his gaze away from Sal and focused on the ocean, which lately seemed to taunt him. Look at me, Doyle, it seemed to say, sympathetically but firmly. Look at all of me. "No!" Doyle responded.

"No what, you don't want to talk to Dr. Owen, or to me?" Sal asked.

A car traveling northbound pulled up to the gas station, and Doyle moved to service. Sal watched him for a moment, then resumed his morning walk.

She answered the phone on the first ring. "Hello?"

"Hello, Mrs. Banks?"

"Yes?"

"My name is Dr. Ralph Owen. I'm a psychiatrist, and I've been treating Mr. Doyle Seeno here in La Sangre, California."

She was silent for a moment. "Oh," she finally said, "poor Doyle."

"Yes, I know what happened to him as a child, and I was given information about the case from the Borden County Sheriff. He didn't give me your contact information but I found you listed."

"Oh that's fine, Doctor. Did the sheriff tell you that that viper who raped Doyle was murdered in prison?"

"Yes, the sheriff told me that."

"Good riddance."

Ralph paused. "As you can imagine, the trauma has been a very hard thing for Doyle to live with."

"I can't even imagine it."

"You're his mother's sister, is that right?"

"Yes."

"The sheriff suggested you might be helpful in telling me something about Doyle's upbringing. He's not forthcoming, and I know his parents are both dead."

"Well sure Doctor, and I'll tell you right off that Wayne, his father, is better off dead. I don't know why my sister married him, I told her not to marry him. I still don't know what she saw in him, but he was—and I say this as a fact, without judgment, because *nobody* liked him—he was a horrible man, a horrible father. I certainly won't even allow Wayne Seeno the description of 'a good old Texas father,' who gave his boy 'a good old Texas beating,' because that would be an insult to Texans, fathers or otherwise."

"So you know that he beat the boy regularly?"

"I certainly do, I even witnessed it a few times, and it was always for the most dumb thing, some silly mistake any child could make. It made me sick, and there was nothing I could do about it. It's not like today, where you can call Child Protective Services and they'll investigate."

"From what you saw, did Wayne use his fists on the boy?"

"No, and that's how Wayne always defended the beatings, saying 'I use my open hands, so it's not a beating.' He thought if he used his fists, then it would be a beating. One time I had the temerity of telling Wayne, 'Was it necessary to beat the poor boy?' But Wayne just replied 'My daddy beat me and made a man out of me! And he always left me on the floor looking up at him.' But Doyle didn't need beatings, he was quiet, sensitive, a loner, not like typical boys, but he was a very good boy. He had a mechanical gift in fact. His father would beat him when Doyle would go into his father's shop and take things apart and put them back together again. Wayne should have seen the boy's mechanical aptitude and encouraged him instead of always putting him down."

"Doyle is the mechanic for us here in La Sangre. He runs the gas station."

"Oh, I'm glad to hear that. I remember he left home to go to an auto mechanic school in El Paso."

"When he graduated from high school?"

"Yes. He couldn't get out of that house fast enough."

Ralph didn't have to take notes, it was classic behavior. "So tell me, what did his mother, your sister, have to say about all this?"

"Well I loved my sister, but she had her own problems. It's funny how different we turned out, and I'm not sure why. But I know she was so afraid of Wayne beating her like he beat Doyle."

"Did he ever?"

"Not that I know of. But anyway she made Doyle the man in her life. She would baby-talk to Doyle when he was a baby, and then a toddler, and I'd say 'Betty, you're going to have to stop baby-talking to Doyle. He's growing up, he wants to be a boy.' But she wouldn't let him grow up! Between his father's beatings and his mother's coddling, I'm surprised the poor boy isn't in an institution. Doctor, she was baby-talking to him as a teenager, all the way to when he left home at 18! He hated it and would tell his mother to shutup, and then his father would beat him for telling his mother to shutup! Poor Doyle was in a lose-lose situation, destroyed both ways."

"Good Lord," Ralph reacted.

"Good Lord indeed, Doctor."

THIRTEEN

December 7, 1984

Dear Ruby,

I know I haven't written for a while, but I've been doing a lot of thinking and figuring on how I'm going to handle the situation with my sister. That newspaper reporter, Nathan Steer, actually stopped by here a couple months ago, asking about Jessie, with some bullshit about an estate she had, like Jessie had anything besides the clothes on her back. Oh I helped her out as much as I could financially, but I didn't really become solvent until our father died, shortly after Jessie died, in a horrible drowning accident in the ocean near his Santa Cruz home, where I now live.

I told you about Bruno, my friend who has been assisting me. He has a friend keeping an eye on Nathan Steer in Santa Rosa, but he sees nothing strange. But you told me that he and his wife recently had dinner with Lillian and her husband, so I think there is something going on, and according to you, Lillian knows everything that happens in La Sangre. So keep watching the both of them, and let me know.

As far as Dr. Owen, I am now convinced that he forced Jessie to have sex with him during the therapy. She couldn't afford to pay him, he was very expensive, like $75 an hour, and I didn't have that much money then, so I believe she had to give him sex as a trade for therapy. Some trade! So I'm sure he was the one responsible for my sister's death. I have filed a complaint with the California Psychiatric Association, and I am waiting for their reply.

Enclosed is another check for $100. As always, I appreciate your discretion about all this.

Maria

It was a beautiful, promising morning on east-bound California 58 just outside Bakersfield. Once Corey got into cruising speed and had secured his position in the freeway's right lane, he beamed into the broadest grin he'd had in six months, since Peter Freeman had come into his life (and left it). "Yes sir! I'm 'Free-man' now!" he shouted above the beautiful sound of his new truck. The whole USA was his, even up the

Alaskan Highway if he wanted.

Corey had sailed through the eight weeks of trucking school, learning the art of driving the big rigs: the 13 gears and how to float them, reading six side-view mirrors, backing up the huge trailers including doubles, handling the 36-inch steering wheel, judging the clearance of the trailers and all 18 wheels around corners and objects, and weight and load balance. Once he got his Class A Commercial Driver's License, Grandma Grace bought him the top-of-the-line Peterbilt 359 Sleeper Truck, complete with shower and multi-speaker tape deck that was now blasting "On The Road Again" by Willie Nelson.

It all started when Grace took him into LFP and introduced him to the shipping department and the dispatchers, and Corey advised them he'll only be submitting bids for long hauls. Grace wasn't shy about introducing Corey as her grandson, in a beat-you-to-it move that would disarm the speculators and also advise the older, seasoned drivers not to mess with or ride her boy. She knew how they could be, but this was Lawrence Freeman Produce after all, and Corey Freeman deserved some respect. The women didn't need to be told to respect Corey, they practically squealed the first time he came into the office. But while he politely responded, Corey wasn't interested. There was something more exciting out there, and he was going to sample it in all 49 continental states.

He found out what was out there on the first day of trucking school, when a scrawny young man with a face like a rat had asked Corey, "So, you looking forward to those lot lizards?"

"Lot lizards?"

The kid looked at Corey like he was from outer space. "Where are you from?"

"Uh, Sacramento."

"Sacramento, huh? Oh there are some great truck stops and rest areas north and south on the I-5, the California 99, and all along I-80! You get to know the girls by name, they give you what you like, no sweat. You just gotta be cool though," the kid looked around and lowered his voice. "Rule Number One, if you're going to go to one of the whore houses in Nevada—they're all across I-80 and US 50, and north and south on the US 95, yeah, it's hog heaven! Anyway, don't *ever* park your truck in front of them, especially carrying for a company like Lawrence Freeman Produce. They're a real conservative company, you're delivering groceries that people eat, right? If someone reports seeing your rig parked next to a whore house, and they complain, bud, you may not ever get another job driving."

"So how do you know all this?" Corey asked. "You're just starting like me."

"My brother's a driver, he's had pussy all

over this country. So anyway, you don't park next to a whore house. Say you want to go to Miss Kitty's on the US 50, you radio them what time you'll be arriving in Carson City, and they'll pick you up in a limo..."

"A limousine?"

"I ain't shittin' you dude, a fuckin' limo! And they take you out there, you do your thing, they got real nice rooms, showers, all of that, and they'll drive you back to your truck."

"So the lot lizards, are they..."

"Oh they're cheap and easy. But be careful of the cops, dude. If a lizard looks *too* good, she could be a cop. All you do is you gotta check out their face. Their bodies are great, but if they don't have that look..."

"What look?"

"The look like they're unhappy and their smile is phony, sometimes their teeth are bad. Even the more expensive ones, who have good teeth, even they can't get rid of that look on their face. So what you do, after you check out their faces and you know they're not cops, just don't look them in the face anymore. Who wants to look at their faces anyway?"

"Not looking at their faces," Corey considered the concept. He and Maria were eye-to-eye—those big brown eyes, they were so deep—the entire two days he spent there.

"No man," the kid said, "avoid the eyes.

You'll see too much." He paused and checked his watch. "Break's over. Don't ever be late for class, either. Oh, one last thing, use a rubber."

Corey followed the kid, his own age actually, back into the classroom, wondering about the lot lizards. Just the term "lot lizards" aroused him. They were out there, on the road, and he'd check them all out.

And now here he was his first day on the road, driving a truck, driving *his* truck, adrenaline surging, with the road as his best friend, and testosterone exploding for some girl who looks just like Maria: tall, toned, firm tits, long dark brown hair, big brown eyes he could get lost in ("Don't look in their eyes, bud."). This first trip was to Salt Lake City, and he had it firmly routed, his Rand McNally Large Scale Motor Carriers Road Atlas on the passenger seat. The first stop would be Sloan, Nevada. He'll park in Sloan and call up for a ride to Pistol Packing Patty's House. Just thinking of it, what it would be like, alighted fuel in his chest and down through his body.

Doyle had known about the adult book store on the old Redwood Highway, just north of Santa Rosa, for as long as he lived in La Sangre. The first time was, of course, by accident when he went to an old garage for a hard-to-find auto part. But after that, whenever he had to go north to Windsor, Healdsburg, or Cloverdale, rather than take the US 101 he took the Old Redwood Highway, slowing down past the yellow cinder-block building whose red sign simply read Adult Books, and below it, Private Video Booths. There were always cars in the parking lot, even early in the morning, and along the frontage one or two semi's would often be parked.

Doyle would wonder and fantasize about who was in that book store, where they came from, what they were looking for, and what they were now doing in there. Since most of the vehicles were pickup trucks he was certain the men in there weren't sissy-fag types, but real men, like his father was. ("Why the hell did I have to get strapped with a sissy boy!" his father complained. "Now Wayne," his mother always responded, "don't talk to the boy like that, he's very sensitive, aren't you Doyle honey?")

Doyle's drive-bys of the adult book store got to be nightly. He'd close up the La Sangre gas station, drive the windy road to Santa Rosa, then go north on the Old Redwood Highway, and when he saw the yellow building, he'd slow down and look. He eventually graduated to pulling into the parking lot and just sitting. He figured that as long as he didn't go *inside* that God forsaken place, he was still all right. He still wasn't queer.

It turned out though that he didn't *have* to go inside. All he had to do was sit there, and men started to approach him, usually asking for a cigarette. Doyle didn't smoke, but he soon bought a pack of Marlboros just so he could offer one to the visitor, and the conversation would go from there.

Doyle knew he was tall, skinny and far from handsome, but he knew he had one thing that most men didn't have, he'd known that since 7th grade when he had to take gym class and use the communal showers. "Donkey Dick Doyle" the other boys pointed and laughed. "Hey Doyle, how much bigger does that thing get when you get a boner? Man, if you ever fucked a chick you'd kill her!" Donkey Dick Doyle quickly became the acronym "DDD," and even more quickly, just "3-D." "Hey Doyle, if you were in 3-D, you know like that movie 'House Of Wax,' your dick would kill the whole audience!" Walking down the halls the boys would call out "Hey 3-D!" ("What's '3-D?'" their girlfriends would ask. "Tell you later baby.")

"How big?" a young man now asked Doyle in the book store parking lot after lighting up the cigarette Doyle had offered him.

"Ten," Doyle said that for first time, his quick response seeming to come from someplace else. It was strange, not himself, this wasn't him. Or *was* it?

"You're shittin' me! Ten? Now, you ain't talking about a Bo Derek '10,' are you, cause you sure ain't that."

"Ten inches."

"Yeah?" The kid's eyes widened. "You got a place we can go?"

"No."

"Follow me." The kid headed to his car.

After the tryst, all Doyle could do was drive back to La Sangre, park behind the gas station, and then stumble over to the church, where he sat down on the steps. He dared not go inside, even though the Pastor always kept it unlocked. The steps were as far as he could go. He hung his head down and asked God, "Why did you let that happen?" As usual, all he heard was the ocean.

A figure was walking south on Highway 1, on his side of the road, a strong walk, arms swinging comfortably. As he neared, Doyle recognized the big man with the red hair, red beard, followed by the Irish Setter.

Him! Satan! God had deserted Doyle for committing the worst sin imaginable, and now Satan was claiming him!

Doyle was certain that if he just went through the doors of the church, Satan couldn't follow him, but he was frozen. It made sense though, now that he committed the unpardonable sin, he couldn't go into the church anyway. He belonged to Satan's legion. Satan was now coming to give his instructions to Doyle, as he probably had to the football player. After all, they had driven into town together, Doyle had seen the two of them riding in the football player's red pickup truck. Now it was Doyle's turn to join the legion.

"Doyle," the man said simply.

"No."

"Doyle, it's okay. We haven't met, but I know you've seen me before. Now, just stay there, don't do anything. I'm going to sit down next to you." The man approached Doyle.

"No!"

"Yes, Doyle. Okay, now try to relax, I'm just going to sit on your left, okay? My dog Barnabas—Barney—is going to sit on your right."

"Oh God, please..."

Jay Carpenter sat next to Doyle, his right shoulder against Doyle's left, his right leg against Doyle's left. "It's okay Doyle, try to relax. I'm just going to put my arm around you, all right?"

"No!"

"Yes," Jay insisted. He put his right arm around Doyle's shoulders, while Barnabas sat on Doyle's right and pressed his body in.

A minute went by.

"Nice," Doyle finally said.

"Yes. It's not sexual, Doyle."

Doyle nodded. "I know."

"Doyle, I want you to look at me."

Doyle didn't respond.

"Now look at me Doyle, you have to."

Doyle turned to the eyes that were beautiful and fathomless. He almost turned away.

"No, don't look away. Just tell me Doyle, what are you looking for? You know what it is, tell me. What are you looking for?"

"I...I don't know."

Sal woke up.

Go to the church Sal.

He didn't hesitate, he grabbed his jeans and shoes, put on his jacket and went to the church.

Not the back door, go to the front.

There Sal saw Doyle sitting alone on the steps, holding his head on his knees.

Oh God, Sal prayed, if I ever needed wisdom and the right words before, in my entire ministry, I need them now.

Sal went over to Doyle's left side and sat next to him, his arm automatically going around Doyle's shoulders.

"Doyle, listen to me. Everyone here, in La Sangre, including and especially me, loves you Doyle. You're reliable, you fix our cars, we depend on you. We're your family."

Doyle looked up at him, his rough, stubbled cheeks wet.

"This is your home," Sal told him.

The lot lizards were more economical, Corey found out, in both money and time, than the houses. Corey would plan his trips accordingly, driving extra hours whenever he could, cheating on his log so he wouldn't get busted. The cops and state patrols were bearing down on independents now, he'd been forewarned in trucking school that they take mileage reports at weigh stations and find out just how long a driver's been at the wheel. Drug tests were taken, but Corey didn't touch drugs and wasn't interested, so he knew he was okay there. However the fines for driving over twelve hours a day could eat up a trucker's profits. Some guys doubled up and drove 24/7, but there was no way Corey would let another man drive his truck. Not ever.

So yeah, the lot lizards fit more neatly into his schedule. They were faster, they knew truckers had tight schedules. On his first overnighter at a truck stop just north of Provo, Utah, he had pulled into a space, did his trailer checks, and once he was settled back in the cab, he got a polite knock on the driver's door.

"Hi! How you doing tonight?" the woman asked him.

(Just check out the face, the kid had told him, make sure she's not a cop, and after that just look to the side, or at their tits, they don't mind that. They don't want to be looked in the face, any more than you want to look at it.)

"Oh, I'm real good now, ma'am," Corey used a rehearsed response, with a fake country twang, and it seem to work.

"Well, I'm glad to hear that! Would you like some company?"

It was only three hours since his 30-minute romp at Pistol Packin' Patty's, but he was ready to go again.

JANUARY - MAY, 1985

FOURTEEN

March 20, 1985

Ms. Maria Malana
PO Box 187
Santa Cruz, CA 95060

RE: Complaint against Dr. Ralph Owen

Dear Ms. Malana,

This letter is pursuant to your complaint against Dr. Ralph Owen, whom you have accused of having sex with your deceased sister, Jessie Malana, while she was under his care, which you believe led to her suicide on June 17, 1984.

We understand your reasons not to meet with us in person nor talk on the phone. Still, as we do with all such charges, we immediately pursued a thorough investigation of Dr. Owen, examining all notes on your sister, interviewing his receptionist, and contacting as many current

and former clients of his as were available.
We were not able to uncover any evidence
of Dr. Owen engaging in any inappropriate
relationship, sexual or otherwise with anyone,
including your sister. We do understand that
Jessie rented Dr. and Mrs. Owen's home in La
Sangre from September 1983 to June 1984,
and that Dr. Owen met with Jessie three times
in Sacramento, where they held sessions at the
hotel he and Mrs. Owen stayed at, but we do not
find any of those events suspicious.

Therefore, at this time we are closing the
file. However, please remember that if you wish
to talk to someone from our office in person, or
if you can provide any evidence that will give
credence to your charge, please let us know and
we will re-open the investigation.

Sincerely,

Dr. Douglas F. Hennessy
Executive Secretary
California Psychiatric Association

March 26, 1985

Dear Ruby,

Read the enclosed letter first.

Can you believe that shit? Look at what some motherfucker wrote from the CPA, better known as the California Psychiatric Assholes! They're all standing up for each other because they're men! If there was a woman involved she'd know how to handle it, I should have requested a woman. But now I'm going all the way to the American Psychiatric Association, I'll demand that a woman assist me, and we'll get that Dr. Owen strung up by the balls. Or maybe I'll just push him off the motherfucking cliff right there at La Sangre, and let the seagulls eat his dick while he's still alive. Sorry Ruby, maybe you better pray for me, ha ha.

You haven't written lately so I guess there's nothing new, but still keep your eyes on that quack shrink, on Lillian, that newspaper man, even his wife, and even Lillian's husband. I think everyone in La Sangre is suspect, except for you. How about the Pastor's wife, what is her name? She probably knows something but you know how that town is, they all band together to protect their own.

I know you're a Christian but you're not like the others, and you'll have to excuse my French but I'm so motherfucking mad.

Those California Psychiatric Assholes aren't through with me yet, not by a long shot.

Destroy both of these letters. Your check is enclosed.

Maria

Corey Freeman, in just a few months, had be-come known at Lawrence Freeman Produce as the fastest, safest, and most reliable independent driver on their books. Most of the other independents, and even the employee drivers, would snub him at the docks and even cry out "Oh, there's Grandma Freeman's golden boy!" but he ignored them. There was no point in reporting any of that behavior to his grandmother, that would just make it worse. He just had to keep on doing what he was doing, using two sets of logs like one of the friendlier drivers had shown him, stressing "Don't you *ever* let it get out that I told the owner's grandson this." In the meantime he was raking in the dough, paying his grandmother off faster than either of them expected.

He stayed with his grandmother rarely now, doing the cross-country routes, coming home just long enough to shower and change and sleep in a regular bed, but a call from the dispatchers would come in—or he'd call them—and he was off again, strategically planning his route. While the lot lizards continued to be expedient to his fast and furious needs, he did have a special lady or two at the houses. After his truck was loaded up, it was just four hours to Sloan for Pistol Packin' Patty's, to be with...damn, what's her name, he almost said Maria! Anyway, from there it was either eastward to Flagstaff, Arizona, which had killer lot lizards at the rest area east of Flag, or north through Nevada to the I-80, then all the way to the eastern seaboard, a hopscotch of lizzies and whores, keeping him energized every 400 miles. Hell, he didn't need any benzos or blues to keep him awake and alert. It was the anticipation, the intrigue, will there be anyone new, any girl he didn't have yet? That's what kept him awake.

Corey was good and he knew it, with gas in the tank, money in his pocket, a rolling home with bed and shower. He was damned good.

"Lillian, I'm scared."

"What Connie?" Lillian looked over at her. They were sitting on the Satoris' deck in the late afternoon. "Is everything's all right with the baby? With Sal?" Sal was inside holding and watching his pride and joy, Freeman Anthony Satori, just one month old.

"Oh no, they're both fine. I'm scared for my other son, Corey."

"Oh." Lillian hesitated. "Have you...heard from him?"

"No, but Grace tells me that he's driving long hours, isn't home for more than a day. He's paying her back: trucking school is paid off and now he's paying her for the truck. He takes routes that others don't want, works holidays—that's why he didn't come home for Thanksgiving and Christmas, or Easter. Which I guess I didn't expect him to. His needing to work to pay off Grace was an excuse, even though Grace has told him he can ease up on payments. And Lillian, Corey's going to get at least a part of his late father's estate, probably a million dollars, so he doesn't have to work so hard. So, everything *seems* okay, but..." she turned to Lillian, "I don't know if I'm ever going to see my child again!"

Lillian lowered her head in deference, and realized she was spending far less time with Connie after she'd started working at the hospital and gotten married. They'd talk after church of course, but Lillian realized she should have *made* the time to spend with Connie. Matthew was working long hours at the kiddieland and making good money. Lillian often joined him after work and assisted him in operating the coaster, saving a few bucks on a ticket-taker and thoroughly enjoying it. Whenever she had Saturdays or Sundays off, she was there with him.

"I guess Corey still needs time," Lillian responded inadequately.

"That's what Grace says, and I'm sure you're both right, but..." Connie turned to the ocean.

"Yes?" Lillian prompted.

"I had a dream the other night. I saw Corey from the back and went up to him, but instead of the yellow blonde hair he's always had, his hair was black. He turned around, and Lillian, he scared me! My own son scared me! His hair was black, his eyebrows, he had a two-day growth of black stubble, and even his blue eyes were black. I said 'Corey, are you okay?' and he nodded but he wouldn't look at me, wouldn't look in my eyes. He just stood there, didn't say anything, his eyes were askew, looking around me, past me."

"None of us have stopped praying for him," Lillian said, feeling even more inadequate.

"Oh, that all seems so useless," Connie said. "I'm tired of it. Am I going to have to go through this with Freeman too? He grows up, runs off, and I'm left home praying for him?"

"Connie, I know it sounds trite but we have to believe that prayer works, believe it in our minds, even if it doesn't *feel* like it's working. But look how we've prayed for Doyle, when he started seeing Dr. Owen, how much better he's gotten. Now Doyle goes into town, drives all the way to Vallejo to see his new girlfriend. And Connie, look at what happened to me. I never expected my prayer to be answered, a prayer that I didn't want to be alone anymore, or if it's meant to be that I'm alone, I'd have peace with that. Connie, do you mind if I pray, right now, for Corey's safety, and for your peace?"

Connie nodded lethargically. "Sure Lillian, go ahead."

Once Doyle started seeing the same men, young and old, tall and short, skinny and fat, at the adult book store on the Old Redwood Highway, he knew it was time for a change. A few of them gave him tips on some other places, adult book stores in San Francisco, and the rest areas up and down US 101, and the new Interstate 280 especially, which had plenty of nice rest areas with large restrooms, landscaped areas with trees and bushes, paths, places to hide, opportunities galore, they advised him. Doyle learned how to act nonchalant like everyone else, and the assignations came quickly and easily. Old "Donkey Dick Doyle" had found his niche, found his place. He was, at long last, popular and liked. He was sure they talked about him favorably.

Doyle never missed church, and everyone noticed how much friendlier he'd become. In the meantime Doyle kept the gas station going, handled the auto repairs and maintenance, and he was even training two willing La Sangre teens who could always use a couple bucks. Moreover, the townspeople were grateful that Doyle was getting out, had a girlfriend. Sal figured the tearful incident that night on the church steps was a one-off, whatever it was.

So Doyle, the church folks would say, it seems that the Lord has finally blessed you with a woman. We're all so happy for you! Have you discussed marriage yet? If you do, you'll get married here in the church, just like Nurse Walker and that husband of hers did. Won't that be nice? When are we going to meet her? Oh, I know it's a long drive from here to Vallejo, and you said she doesn't have a car, but maybe some weekend you can bring her for church. She can stay at our home for the weekend, so everything is proper. Praise the Lord!

"Sal?" Matthew said softly, not wanting to wake him if he was asleep in his deck chair. It was late afternoon.

Sal lifted his head immediately. "Yeah? Oh hi Matt."

"I didn't want to wake you."

"No, come on up," Sal motioned to the chair next to him.

"I uh..." Matthew began, unsure as he sat down. "I don't know exactly how to say this, but..."

"You want something to drink? Coffee? Iced tea?"

"No, I'm good. Let me just come right out and say it."

Sal nodded and waited.

"Well, I've been living here in La Sangre for eight months now, and...you know, I've tried to talk to the men, but I can't get anywhere with them. They're cold and look down on me; I'm not the paranoid type but I'm sure it's because of my carnival background. Or if they do talk, everything is about God and scripture, like they're trying to save me, as if I'm not already because I don't act like them. I'm sorry to say this Pastor, but they can really piss me off."

Sal gave a chuckle. "I know what you mean. I can't have any conversations with them either, but it's different with me, it's an occupational hazard. For a while now, I've been talking to Ralph...."

"Dr. Owen?"

"Yeah. He's all right. He and I are pretty much in the same line of work; he said that outside of the office, people are afraid that he's observing everything they say and every move they make."

They were quiet until Sal said, "You sure you don't want some coffee? It's on."

"Well, yeah, sure, if it's on. Black."

While Sal went in the house Matthew enjoyed the panoramic view the Satoris had of the Pacific. It stirred his wanderlust a bit, but not much; that nag of the road was now tempered by the joy of finally having a wife and home.

"Here you go," Sal handed him a steaming mug. "So let's talk."

"All right, what about?"

"Anything. You go first. I've been wanting to hear some stories of the road."

Matthew sipped his coffee and grinned. "Yeah, the road. I was just thinking about that. I miss it sometimes, but it was time to settle down."

"Never mind that, tell me a story of the road."

"Sure. I have a lot of them. One time, before I had my own Miler coaster, I was a roustabout for the West Coast Shows..."

"Roustabout?"

"A carny who doesn't own his own ride, works directly for the show, does everything. So we were doing a show in Medford, Oregon, and I was working the Paratrooper. So this girl, early twenties, real cute, gets on the ride with a paper dress!"

"Oh yeah! Those were a fad in the...early 70s I think."

"Right. So as I'm latching her in, I say 'Are you sure you want to ride this in that dress?' And she said 'I just rode the Tilt-A-Whirl and I didn't have any problem!' I said 'But that's an enclosed ride,' but then she started in with the 70s feminist thing, 'I'm a feminist and I can wear whatever I want!'"

"Oh brother...."

"I know. So I started up the ride and guess what happened?"

"You don't mean...."

"You know Bruno, I've been thinking," Maria broke their silence, sitting together on the deck of her Waddell Beach home.

"Yeah?" Bruno looked up. He was in his red beach trunks, leggings pulled up to his crotch to get the proper tan lines.

"Well, the California Psychiatric Assholes fucked me over with their bullshit, and now the American Psychiatric Assholes say they support the California Assholes' findings! All those fucking men! It's time I took things into my own hands."

"With my help of course."

"With your help, always."

Bruno looked at her expectantly. She was wearing a bikini, her long bronze body gracing the deck chair. ("With your help always," she just said. She said something nice to him.) "Maria..." he began, but his yearning tone gave him away.

"Oh Brutus, please don't start again!"

"How many times have I told you not to call me that!"

"Well it's the only way I can get you to snap out of it! I don't love you Bruno, I never will. I can't, don't you understand that? I appreciate what you've done for me..."

"*Appreciate* it? That I murdered your father for you?"

"You didn't *murder* him, you *executed* him, a man who fucked me, his own daughter, and when I had the baby HE FUCKED HER AT EIGHT YEARS OLD! HOW FAR WAS THAT MONSTER GOING TO GO? WAS HE GOING TO START HANGING AROUND ELEMENTARY SCHOOLS NEXT?"

"Maria," Bruno attempted, again, "you told me you didn't report it to the police. Why didn't you...."

"BECAUSE I LIKED IT BRUTUS! I *LIKED* THE SEX. AND I LOVED MY FATHER! HE WAS SUCH A TALL, HANDSOME MAN IN HIS 3-PIECE LAWYER'S SUIT! I USED TO WATCH HIM IN COURT. HE WAS BETTER THAN PERRY MASON! AND I HATED HIM! I LOVED HIM AND I HATED HIM! NOW HOW AM I GOING TO REPORT *THAT* TO THE POLICE!"

Silence.

Bruno hated it when Maria went crazy like this, but he decided to pursue it. Maybe...maybe he could reach her. "But...but when you got pregnant, how did you...."

Maria cooled down quickly; somehow she was always able to do that. She couldn't control her explosions of rage, but she could cool down quickly. "My father, the hot-shot San Francisco lawyer handled all that. We lived up there—we only came here on weekends—and he coached me on a story of some boy that I had sex with and he disappeared. He knew better than to make up a rape, because there'd be a police investigation. So he put Father Unknown on Jessie's birth certificate."

"What about your mother?"

"Her? She left us both when I got pregnant. She took her million dollars, signed, and split. I don't know where that bitch is."

Bruno looked down. He wanted her to know he loved her, and that he wasn't stupid. She met him a year ago when he was a bouncer at the Saddle Rack Country Bar in San Jose. He quit when she hired him to...God could he say it? To kill her father. And he's hung around since then, her friend and protector, the one man who would be kind to her, take care of her.

"Why is it so hard," Maria wondered, as she had all her life, "for people to understand? Like a wild animal I was caught, and I was bought."

"Bought?"

"He bought me a brand new Datsun 280Z when I turned 16. I loved that car, and I loved him—I *thought* I loved him—for giving it to me. That black Maserati that Jessie killed herself in, he bought that on *her* sixteenth birthday." She turned to Bruno. "Why is it so hard for people to understand? After Jessie killed herself, I knew the only way I'd have any freedom was to kill my father. Bruno, you made the world a safer place, or the Bay Area at least. Why is it so difficult for people to understand that? Am I all alone here or what?"

She turned back to the ocean.

Bruno looked at her. "I understand it, Maria. I'm not as dumb as you think I am. And you're not alone here, you have me."

"All right, I'm sorry," she sighed. "You know how I get when I think of all that. But Bruno, my dear friend, please understand. This is the way I am, and I'll never be able to love you the way you want me to, or anyone else. And I'm not a lesbian either, because you know I tried that, and they're worse than men! They keep trying to," she shivered, "*touch* me."

"Maria, listen to me. I killed...executed... your father because I love you."

"And you loved the $50,000 that you don't have to report to the IRS?"

"Maria, don't! I'm serious! You were so... unhappy, lonely, angry, when Jessie died last year, that I thought with your father finally out of your life forever, you'd be free to start a new life, forget the past, start loving again...."

"Loving *again*? I have *never* loved!"

"Okay, you can start with loving me. You know I'll be patient with you, I always have been. But with each thing that's happened, Jessie's death, your father's execution, that thing with the preacher's son...."

"Oh I fucked that boy because I hated him, hated everything he stood for. I wanted to fuck some hate into him, and I hope I did. And I'll do that again, with anyone, man or woman, if I have to, starting with...." She stopped.

"What?" Bruno looked at her. It's not over, he knew, and a chilling omen was that it may never be over.

"I want that La Sangre shrink, Bruno. I don't know if I'm going to just fuck him and destroy his marriage, or..."

"The badger game? Are you going to go that low?"

"Oh yeah, like that's lower than murder?" Maria scoffed.

"Execution you said. But what I'm trying to say is, now you're going after the shrink. They completed an investigation on him...."

"All fucking lies!"

"Maria, baby...."

"Don't call me baby!"

Bruno fought for a proper term of endearment, but there was none. "Maria, you're just getting worse, you want to destroy everyone." Bruno lowered his tone. "Even me I think."

"Oh no Bruno, not you. But hear me out, what you're saying may be true, but let's do just one more, okay baby? Maybe then, when they're all gone or locked up, all those sick evil men, I can start again. What do you say?"

"Oh God..." was all he could manage.

"Don't start with that God shit. Are you with me or aren't you?"

He couldn't do it again. Even the "execution" excuse fell flat. He had murdered a man, period, and he had to live with the nightmares of her father's eyes bulging out of their sockets as he squeezed. "I love you," was all Bruno could manage.

"I know you do, Bruno. Okay, it's settled then." She stood up and slipped her bikini top off, then wiggled out of the bottoms. "How about a swim?"

Sal and Ralph had taken to regular afternoon visits on either Sal's deck or Ralph's front porch, where Sal drank coffee and Ralph drank wine or smoked his pipe.

"Well Doctor, I've got a recurring dream I need you to look at. How much will that set me back?"

Ralph gave a chuckle. "For you, no time or charges."

"Thanks."

Sal told Ralph about his dream, the fissures between his father, even Jay, but no fissure between him and Jessie—whose name he conveniently changed to Doris—and the dream ending with Jay saying "Run and jump Sal!"

"First of all," Ralph began, "I like what your father said. He meant well not encouraging your going into the ministry. I feel that way about psychiatry. I told my own kids to stay out of it, though now I think they could both use a little shrinking. But as far as reaching people, I'll bet my percentage of conversions—where patients start growing up—is about as low as your salvation rate. I just make a lot more money doing what I do. But like you, I'm a threat to them."

"Is that what you think I am to others? A threat?"

"Of course you are! You make people look at themselves. You're not a threat to me, because I know who I am and what I believe. Same with you. But do you think either of us are able to go around making friends? Even us shrinks can't get together, to golf or just bullshit; we always talk about our work, and you can get tired of that."

They sat quietly for a few minutes.

"Anyway," Ralph continued, "you obviously have a connection with that lady, Doris, and that's not unusual. We men store tapes in our brain, our very own personal video collection, and they come up at the most inopportune times...and I should know Sal, even headshrinkers have to deal with that."

Sal looked at him.

"Oh no Sal, we're in shrink-client mode right now, no personal experiences from me, let's just say I can relate. Now, the Jay Carpenter thing is a no-brainer, even I know who He is, and the run-and-jump bit, don't you believers tell each other to 'take a leap of faith?'"

Sal mulled it over. "I thought I had taken that leap. Maybe I haven't yet." He waited for Ralph to respond.

"Session's over." Ralph raised his wine glass in toast.

Bruno and Maria dried off on the deck. He loved to look at her, he could do it 24/7. "I love you. And you can't stop me from saying that."

"All right, I won't." She lifted her right leg onto the deck chair and began drying it.

"So," she said matter-of-factly, "through my contact in La Sangre, I'm going to find out about Dr. Owen's habits and practices, how often his wife goes into Santa Rosa. Then we can schedule a time when she's gone, to do what we're going to do." She started drying her left leg, moved up to her buttocks and her private area, up to her stomach.

She always dries off from the bottom up, Bruno smiled to himself. It's one of the things that made her different from all the other woman he'd known. And there were many. All beautiful. It was as easy as walking into a singles bar wearing Jordache Jeans for Men, snakeskin cowboy boots, a half-buttoned fitted white shirt, a gold crucifix mixed in with chest hair when he didn't shave, and a sky-blue sport jacket to bring out his eyes.

But for now there will be no other women. He'll need no other woman. Not after he's had Maria.

Maria moved the towel upward. "Maybe he has a girlfriend," she pondered. "You can have your buddy up in Santa Rosa, what's his name?"

"Shawn." Bruno watched her dry her breasts.

"Shawn. He can follow the doctor, see if he meets a girlfriend somewhere." She put the towel around her shoulders and paused thoughtfully. "But blackmail of course is out. My father—God I hate that word—left millions for me and Jessie. If only she hadn't...." she faltered. "I was just too late to do what had to be done."

Exactly *who* did it, Maria, Bruno thought, but he kept silent.

"Anyway Bruno, you and I are going to have to deal with the good doctor directly." She looked at him with her big brown eyes, salt water residue still on her full lips. "Permanently."

"You mean..."

"Yes, permanently."

"Again?"

"Again."

He looked at her: nude and beautiful and glowing against the impending sunset, and began to grow erect, as always.

Yes, Maria was a promise he would kill for again.

"I love you," he spoke from the heart.

JUNE 1 TO FATHER'S DAY, 1985

FIFTEEN

THE SECRET OF LA SANGRE

by Anne P. Owen

CHAPTER 4

The ladies loved to get together, to talk, pray, and gossip, and it was often hard to know which one they were doing. They also gorged themselves on sugary items which kept most of them somewhere between overweight and obese, more on the latter side, while they derided the evils of alcohol, specifically mentioning the psychiatrist and his wife drinking wine on their porch at sunset, and Nurse Walker's new husband—a very strange and even mean man, they decided—was once seen on his porch with a short, clear glass full of ice cubes and a light brown liquor that the women were certain wasn't iced tea. Worse, he was often not wearing a shirt!

They then prayed for his salvation, and when they were through, they attacked a plate of fresh dipped Ghirardelli Square chocolates that one of them had splurged on during her last trip into San Francisco.

"Ghirardelli must be a Christian company," one of them said as she wiped cherry cream off her lip. "I mean to be able to make something so wonderful."

"Yes," another agreed, "this truly is the Lord at work."

"Amen."

Well, that was a good start for the day, Anne decided. She was getting better, using more different types of words and phrases, mostly from the thesaurus Ralph had bought her so she could find better words, but of course then she had to look some of them up in the dictionary to see what they meant. So, she kept both the thesaurus and the dictionary sitting right next to her typewriter on the kitchen table, only to be moved for meals.

From where she sat in the kitchen, Anne could hear Ralph typing away in his office. She giggled. The family that *writes* together stays together! Hey, that was good! She'll use that somewhere in her book.

Anne knew that Ralph understood that they're each writing for different audiences, and would never share the same space in a book store, so it wouldn't affect their marriage, it would make it even stronger, and they could appear together on the TV talk shows, him giving the psychiatric view of La Sangre, while she gave a woman's point of view. They would complement each other, and Ralph would be so proud of her.

While she doubted she'd ever be able to fathom all the medical terms and details of his book, she was curious what he was writing this very minute. What *could* he write, she suddenly wondered? She was the one who had infiltrated the ladies, getting to know them and finding out what makes them tick, like the American spies in Germany during World War II that her husband would tell her about, how they learned to speak German without an accent. Isn't that just what she was doing here in La Sangre? Like a foreign language—Christianese, she decided—she was learning how to frame everything with "The Lord this" and "The Lord that." She had concocted a story when they asked her how long she had been saved. "Oh, I was doing a lot of sinful things," she would explain, "and I discovered the error of my ways when I was in my twenties and saw the movie 'The Greatest Story Ever Told,' and, well, here I am!" But she was stumped when they pressed her on what "sinful things" she had been doing. She couldn't think of any.

Oopsie! She'd gotten pregnant two months before they got married. As you did in those days, she told everyone that their 8-pound baby was born two months premature. Which part of that was a sin? The pre-marital sex? They got married, after all. Lying about her term of pregnancy? She didn't know whether either or both of these were sins. But she doubted that the other women—who would readily say both were sins—really knew either.

Anne was wondering if she should put that quandary in her book—it was very *Peyton Place*—when the typing from Ralph's office suddenly stopped, jolting her from her reverie. What *was* Ralph writing, anyway?

June 1, 1985

Dr. Douglas F. Hennessy
Executive Secretary
California Psychiatric Association

Dear Dr. Hennessy:

Enclosed are xeroxes of the threatening letters mentioned in my last letter. I'm keeping the originals; if I file a complaint with the police they'd want to study the originals.

As you can see, the postmarks are various; no longer just Santa Cruz, but San Jose, San Francisco, Morgan Hill, Monterey, all in the same area of course and, it's obvious, from the same person. As I say, I'm not sure if or when I'll go to the police, but I appreciate your re-opening the file regarding my alleged—and certainly untrue—sexual abuse of my patient Jessie Malana, so that the perpetrator may hopefully be exposed and appropriately dealt with.

I'm starting to feel uncomfortable with the frequency and intensity of these letters, not really frightened but certainly uncomfortable.

I will let you know if I decide to involve the police, and will put the two of you together.

Sincerely,

Ralph Owen M.D.
Psychiatrist
La Sangre, California

The rest area wasn't very busy this evening. A few cars and trucks were driving in and out, but they went into and out of the rest room for its intended purpose; nobody was casually strolling around. Doyle was ready to drive to the next rest area further down the I-280 when he saw someone get out of a semi and head into the restroom. A big guy, he looked good from the back, had a confident walk, looked promising. Doyle went into the restroom where the man was using one of the urinals. Oh no, it was....

"Doyle," Jay turned to him as he urinated. "Be honest with me, and with yourself. What are you really looking for here?"

That same question, as before, put Doyle on the very edge of his truth. Just one more step.

"What are you looking for, Doyle?" Jay repeated.

"Myself."

"Hi Grace."

"Oh hi Connie, so nice of you to call. How are you?"

"Well..." Connie hated calling Grace for her worries about Corey, when here's a woman who lost her husband and son, and it was always Grace being the strong one.

"Oh Grace...please, tell me how *you're* doing, for a change."

Grace chuckled. "I still have some good days and some bad days, but I'm doing more with the business now, attending the board meetings, even making some company decisions, so that keeps me busy. Then there's the grandkids."

"Oh I'm glad, Grace. I'm afraid I have selfish reasons for calling, as always."

"Never mind that, just tell me."

"I had that dream again, about Corey having black hair and not looking me in the eye. Have you noticed, as far as you can tell, is he okay?"

"Well, he still has his blonde hair, of course. It's down to his shoulders, and he's making a poor attempt at a beard, his father was hairier than Corey and had a full beard by eighteen."

You're telling me, Connie smiled to herself.

"As far as any behavior, nothing really errant that I can see. He doesn't spend much time at... much time here. He'll stay for a day or two, sometimes we'll go to one of my daughters' homes for a family meal, but then he takes off. Once he took the grandkids to Magic Mountain, but otherwise he just rests up around the pool. He offers to do chores, but I have help for that. He doesn't lie to me, and I don't want or need to know anything. I went through it with Peter, a young man's business is his own. Peter had a girl living with him while he was playing with the Forty-Niners. Very pretty girl, very *nice* girl, but she moved out when he retired, looking for an active football player, I'm sure. Frankly, I was relieved."

"Well, as long as you're confident Corey's not being...self destructive."

"Well I can tell you he's not into alcohol, I'd know it when he's here. And as far as any drugs, Lawrence Freeman Produce does drug testing for not only employees but the contractors, and if he came up positive with anything, I'd know about it. He's definitely clean."

"Thank God. And thank you Grace."

"You're welcome. And Connie, I know, it's

very hard to be patient and let go."

"I'm doing my best."

"I know you are."

Corey's anticipation was pumping up with each mile eastward across Kansas from Topeka to Salina. This pounding rush he now understood was at least half of the fun, half of the fix that raced through his bloodstream. He ejected the cassette tape of Eddie Rabbitt's "Drivin' My Life Away" so he could concentrate on the thumping that ran through his chest, down his legs, throughout his body. As long as it didn't interfere with his driving, he was good. He had another 50 miles to enjoy his powerful manhood, but man, it would be even better once he arrived. The second half was even more powerful than the anticipation.

Salina, Kansas was his favorite stop, located in the very center of the continental U.S. It's where he met Sabrina. "Sabrina from Salina" he called her. Good at her game, Sabrina didn't tell Corey that she wasn't from Salina. That was the fantasy he was paying her good money for. On their last visit, a mere five days ago on his eastward crossing, he'd given her three hundred dollars to buy a long, flowing dark-brown wig, and he couldn't wait to see her in it. "Sabrina from Salina, the Lizzie at Edie's Truck Stop!" he sang out tunelessly, and then laughed at himself and shoved the Eddie Rabbitt tape back in.

He'd radioed ahead to the Lot Lizard connection in Salina, advising when he'd be arriving at Edie's, and to alert Sabrina he'd be right on time, with a few minutes prior for a stop in the cafe for a few cups of coffee. No food, that came afterward, when he'd drive another 200 miles to Mack's Truck Stop in Colby, Kansas, his hunger for food fueling him there just like the sex had fueled him to Salina. He'd eat and sleep at Mack's, tying a blue rag to the driver door handle, signally the lizzies that "Don't come a-knockin', I'm a-sleepin'."

Corey's life as a trucker was planned and executed down to the second. His new truck never had a breakdown, he stayed on top of its maintenance, and he was making great money. The way he was going he'd have Grandma paid off within two years. He offered his grandma money for his bedroom (his old man's bedroom, Pete Freeman of the San Francisco Forty-Niners!) but she refused, saying it was part of their deal. He had no overhead, other than the money he spent for his Lot Lizzie Lovin', and his cheap meals at the diners.

"Hi Corey!" Vivian greeted him in Edie's Cafe. Fat, bottle-blonde Vivian was yet another of his favorite en route people; always cheerful, a great sense of humor, greeting him by name, always taking care of him, always "leaving the light on" for him. It sometimes occurred to him that the over-tipping he did for Vivian and all the other waitresses from Bakersfield to Boston may have been the reason for their warm engagement, but he didn't care.

"Just coffee, Viv." He sat down at a stool. "What's new?"

"Well," she paused, holding the coffee pot, "since I saw you last week my youngest, Janelle, finally had her second baby, a little boy. Eight pounds!"

"Congratulations Grandma!"

"Thank you! It's our first boy in the family! Duke is so proud. I told him that this makes up for me only giving him girls. Duke said a grandson is almost as good as a son, and he's hoping he'll grow up to be a trucker like his granddaddy."

"What's his name?"

"Well, Janelle had no choice but to name him after her husband, Roy, but she said we can nickname him Duke." She poured coffee into Corey's mug, leaving plenty of room, from experience.

"Well, I'm sure he'll become a great driver." Corey filled the rest of the mug with half-and-half and took a sip. Ah, good. He needed that. He took a cursory glance around the diner, mostly truckers, all gabbing, looking and sounding wired. Corey was rightly smug, watching them. He didn't need any amphetamines, Benzedrine, and even cocaine like most of those drivers do. All he needed was his coffee. Coffee was legal, he was no drug addict like them. He worked hard, was never late for a load, never had an accident.

Vivian took the coffee pot further down the counter for refills and to check on everyone else. When she returned she saw the front door open.

"Well Jay!" she cried. "You handsome man, long time no see! I thought you didn't love me anymore!"

He came over to where she was standing next to Corey. "Now Vivian," he admonished her gently, "you know you're my favorite girl on the I-70!" He leaned over the counter and gave her a peck on the lips.

Vivian smiled lovingly at him. She raised the pot, "Coffee?"

There were three empty stools to Corey's left, but Jay made a point of sitting on the one next to Corey.

"Not just yet Hon, I have to talk to this young man." Jay turned to Corey. "Finish your coffee," he said firmly.

"What?" Corey asked surprised. He recognized Jay, but he couldn't remember where...oh yeah, last Father's Day.

"Corey," Vivian raised her eyebrows, "sounds to me like you're going to get a lecture, honey."

"On second thought, forget the coffee," Jay ordered. He fished in his pocket for a five dollar bill and lay it on the counter. "Come on outside, so we don't have to disrupt the paying customers."

Corey set his mug on the counter with a thud and looked at Vivian for help.

"Just go," she told him, giving him a firm motherly look.

"Let's walk to your truck," Jay said once they were outside.

"Uh...over there," Corey pointed. Jay was totally different from how Corey remembered him that morning when he gently and firmly set Corey's broken leg.

"Enough is enough," Jay said as they walked. "Now you're going to get in your truck, drive to Colby—you don't need coffee right now—and eat and sleep there, *with* the blue rag on the door handle."

"But I'm..."

"I know what you want to do, but like I said, enough is enough. Now, when you get back to Bakersfield, you're going to go to Sex Addicts Anonymous, they meet nightly in the Bakersfield VFW, the one on Wilson Road."

"I don't think..."

"You don't think you're an addict? Because you have it so methodically detailed and never miss a delivery, you think you're not an addict? You think you're just a young man getting his licks in? How do you think addiction starts?"

They arrived at Corey's truck. "Now, get in and drive."

"Jay!" a woman's voice cried out.

Jay and Corey turned, as Sabrina walked towards them, carrying a long, flowing, dark brown wig. "Jay!" she said again and ran up to him, hugging him, ignoring Corey. "Oh, how I've missed you."

Jay put his arms around her. "I've missed you too, Margaret."

She looked up at Jay's face. "Can we talk?"

"Of course we can. I'm just sending Corey on his way."

"Here Corey," she threw the brown wig at him. "I don't think I'll be needing this tonight... maybe not ever."

"Jay?" Corey was rejected, by a girl whose name wasn't Sabrina and, apparently, by Jay.

"I just have one last thing to say to you, Corey, before it's too late." Jay pressed his forefinger against Corey's sternum. "Get your ass home." He turned Margaret around and they walked off, his arm around her shoulders. But then he turned and yelled back to Corey, "And I don't mean Bakersfield!"

Corey was left standing by his truck, holding the dark-brown wig.

SIXTEEN

"Hey Bruno."

"Yeah Shawn. Whattaya got?"

"Well I think that shrink Owen is a real square. I've been on his tail, and that guy has no girlfriends. If you saw what his wife looks like, you'd think he would. The wildest thing they do, according to Ruby, is drink wine on their porch in the evening. Ruby says that gets those Christian tongues wagging."

"I'll bet. So did you buy Ruby dinner?"

"Just like she wanted, at The Tides. She sprayed me with lobster juice as she chowed down on that thing, like it was going to come back alive any minute and eat *her*. By the way Bruno, she made me give her a hundred dollars, besides dinner."

"Jesus. Maria just put a check in the mail for her. Well, add it to your expenses."

"That reminds me, Ruby managed to get a photo of Dr. Owen, she's very proud of that, a regular Emma Peel she thinks she is. It's a clear photo, I put it in the mail. He's not bad looking, decent shape, big guy, even bigger than that crazy pastor."

"The bigger they are...."

"The harder they fall, check." Shawn paused. "So, you want me to stay on him?"

"Yeah, just in case something strange happens. Maria and I have to decide how we'll handle it."

"And I don't want to know."

June 3, 1985

Dear Maria,

I was just thinking about a way you can be alone to talk with Dr. Owen. The Sunday after next is Father's Day. Even though we won't have the church picnic this year, Father's Day a big thing here in La Sangre, almost as big as Christmas. Everyone spends Friday night and Saturday getting ready for it. Saturday evening me and some of the other ladies will be cleaning and decorating the church. I already asked Anne Owen to join us and she said she will. That way I'll keep her busy so that you have a chance to be alone with Dr. Owen and talk to him.

I'm glad you'll be able to work things out with him, what with losing your Jessie. Maybe he'll be able to give you some more information on her so you can rest easily.

By the way, Dr. Owen is actually a nice man. We all thought he and his wife were stuck up, because they never joined in before. And if you can believe it, they're actually going to church together, every Sunday morning. Everyone is praying against the demon of psychiatry, so we're hoping he'll get another profession. Maybe Pastor Satori can give him a job like he did with your Jessie at the Saloon. The cook needs help in the kitchen, especially with summer here.

As you might know, I had a date with Shawn last night at The Tides. He's really cute, a lot cuter than that skinny, ugly newspaperman. Just let me know if you want me to get more out of him.

Love,

Ruby

"Hi, I'm Randy. And I'm a sex addict."

"Hi Randy," the men raised their hands in unison.

Corey looked around at them, eight including himself, seated in a circle in uncomfortable steel folding chairs. All ages. Six of them were like him, dressed like blue-collar workers, the other two wore dress shirts, their ties loosened.

"I guess I had to," Randy paused nervously, "go all the way down to the bottom, two weeks ago, when I realized I had spent so much money on 'Call A Chick' that, God, I didn't have money for the mortgage! I'd maxed out my credit card, I couldn't use that. This was my fucking mortgage for chrissake! For the house that my wife and kids LIVE IN! And I did that for some girl named Lorena! I actually believed that she waited for me to call, enjoyed talking to me, that she...LOVED ME!" He took a breath. "I thought I was so clever, waiting until the wife and kids were asleep, using my private line in my office in the garage so they couldn't hear me, lying that I was working...paying three dollars a minute for two-hour phone calls, at least five days a week!" He looked around at the other men. "And you know what, for all my fantasies, I'll bet she was as fat as a hog and had a face like a horse!"

The men chuckled, two of them raising their hands in silent agreement.

"Thank you." Randy sat down.

Another man stood up.

"Hi, I'm Stan. And I'm a sex addict."

"Hi Stan."

"I just realized that it's not the ...not the sex that I'm addicted to so much as what you guys call the intrigue. Thinking about it, searching for it, will she or won't she, what would it be like with this one or that one, all the thinking, the planning, the lying, spending the money, doing all that and *wondering* and *fantasizing* about what *might* happen, that's the part that's exciting to me, because if and when I do...complete it, it's never that good, and that makes me think 'Well maybe the next time will be better.' And there's always one more, always the one girl that's eluded me, that will be prettier, better body, firmer tits and ass, just perfect. And that's what I'm addicted to, that there's always going to be one more." He sat down.

Oh hell, why not? Corey stood up. "Hi, I'm Corey. And I'm a sex addict."

"Hi Corey."

Before he stood up, all he knew to say was that he was a sex addict. What *else* could he say, this early in the game? Nevertheless, he found himself talking.

"Well I'll tell you guys one thing," he pointed at the seven men. "I enjoyed every fucking minute of it! I won't take that back! I'm not going to slobber and cry and say I regret it, because I fucking *loved* it! It felt good, it was fun, and I'm fucking lucky—thank you Jesus—that I didn't get rolled and stabbed by one of those lot lizards! So right now that's all I have to say to you assholes." He sat down.

The room erupted with The Great Laughter, that went past the closed door and resounded through the empty halls of the Veterans of Foreign Wars building in Bakersfield, California.

Corey didn't request or accept any loads for a week, staying at his Grandmother's house, sleeping in his Dad's bed, visiting his four aunts and their husbands, playing with his young cousins, who adored him. In the desk in his bedroom, he found a book of poetry his father had written. He wondered if Grandma knew about it, she probably did. She would have had to go through Peter's things after his death, but neither of them said anything to each other about his poetry book.

One page simply had a title on it with no poetry, "My Father, My Self, My Son, My Soul." Or maybe that was the entire poem.

Another page had only one word, "Connie."

"Hi Vince, it's Corey," he said to the LFP dispatcher. "Do you have anything going up the 101 in California?" ("Get your ass home Corey. And I don't mean Bakersfield.")

"In fact I do, Corey, day after tomorrow, up to Eureka."

"That's perfect. Single or doubles?"

"Single. They want delivery Monday morning. That's the day after Father's Day, is that all right? You doing anything over that holiday weekend?"

"No, that's perfect. Thanks Vince."

June 6, 1985

Dear Ruby,

Thank you for the latest information. I think it's a good idea that I meet with Dr. Owen on Saturday night as you suggest. I don't know yet what time I'll be there, but after it gets dark. You said you can keep Mrs. Owen busy, please do so in any way you can. But if something strange happens or changes, give me a call— and remember only call me if it's absolutely necessary—at the Bodega Bay Lodge. I don't have the number on me but you can find it. I'll be registered under the name of Jessie Freeman.

Maria

On Saturday, June 15, at 6 AM at the LFP loading dock, Corey hooked his truck onto the loaded trailer for the haul to Eureka. He had a new plan of travel, thanks to a few meetings with Sex Addicts Anonymous. No more whore houses—not that there were any along the route from Bakersfield to Eureka—and no more lot lizards. He was through with that. Porn was good enough; cheap, easy, fast, it gave him his fix like methadone to a recovering heroine addict. Besides, with porn, who was he hurting? He'd drive up the 99 to Fresno, park his rig at the truck stop, and take a taxi to an adult book store that had private viewing booths. Any taxi driver knew where everything was, they worked with truckers all the time. So everything was all right, nice and easy, and he'd be making better time than before, in addition to spending less money.

Sal and Ralph were having their morning coffee on Ralph's porch, chatting idly, when Matthew walked up.

"Hey Matt," Sal greeted him, surprised.

"Let me grab you a chair." Ralph went inside to the kitchen. "Annie, would you bring some coffee to the porch for Matt?"

"Matt? You mean Matthew?" she looked at him, surprised. "Oh, of course. Does he want cream or sugar?"

Ralph took a kitchen chair out to the porch. "Here Matt, sit. Cream and sugar in your coffee?"

"Just black, thanks."

"Black!" Ralph called back to the kitchen.

"On the road I used to take cream and sugar to kill the taste of road house coffee, but La Sangre coffee is always very good, whoever makes it."

"Yeah, that's one thing we teetotalers do well," Sal quipped, "is make good coffee."

Anne came out with a steaming mug. "Here you go Matthew!" This was a first, Matthew coming over for coffee, all three men spending time together beyond a few words after church. She would have liked to join them—this would be a good chapter for her book, which was moving along nicely—but she figured she could hear them well enough from inside.

"Thanks Anne," Matthew nodded to her.

"You're very welcome. Nice to have you here." She went back inside and straight to her typewriter on the kitchen table, while Ralph, Sal, and Matt sipped and enjoyed easy conversation.

After a brief, cold morning swim in the ocean, Maria got in the shower, during which she decided she and Bruno would drive up Highway 1 from Waddell Beach to San Francisco, rather than take the I-280. It promised to be a nice morning, and she'd have Bruno drive so she could relax and think about what she would be doing tonight, how she and Bruno would get to Dr. Ralph Owen so she could make the final confrontation. It was the last thing she had to do and, as Bruno said, she'll be free. Then the world would be hers.

She put her face up to the shower head, inviting its warm water into herself. Maybe she could even love Bruno if she wanted, she didn't know; maybe, maybe not. The thought of sex with him still wasn't appealing. But that might change. The whole point was that she'd finally be free to live her life. She was just 40, still beautiful, she didn't even need to color her hair yet. It all felt right, this was her time, finally. Jessie would be avenged, Maria would have completed her duty to her little sister, her daughter, and the world would be hers, with whatever and whomever she wanted.

Maria Carlotta Malana will finally arrive.

Corey made a starchy grin in the back seat of the Fresno taxi as it took him back to his truck. He had only been in the book store a half hour, and the images gave him a warm sense of comfort, of well being. Yeah, this would work fine, just a fast stop, a quick fix, and on his way again. Nothing wrong with this. Nothing he has to confess to those losers at SAA. No more brown wigs to buy, no more sad and sorry women to look at... not that he ever looked in their eyes. ("Don't look in their eyes, you see too much.") Corey was just going to make more money, maybe even buy a house in Bakersfield, where his new family was.

("Get your ass home, Corey. And I don't mean Bakersfield!")

Corey curled his lip. Sure, he'd requested a route that would take him through Santa Rosa, but for now, that's as close as he'll get to La Sangre. "We'll just wait and see what happens," Corey mumbled aloud.

"Como Señor?" the cab driver asked.

"Oh. Siento. Nada."

After finishing his coffee and all three agreeing to make this a regular thing, switching off homes, Matt excused himself from Ralph and Sal to head off to work. Sal thought about taking his leave, but decided to stay awhile.

Two seagulls were on the roof of the neighboring house, fighting over a catch.

"The seagulls seem noisier lately, more aggressive," Ralph commented.

"Yeah, I've noticed that too." Sal paused. "Say Ralph, I've wanted to ask you something for a long time."

"Yeah?"

"Well, what's it like, being an atheist?"

It was a hard and fair question, Ralph allowed. "I don't know, Sal. I don't know that I ever really thought about what it's *like*. I just do it. But I'll say one thing, based on everything I've seen, not just here in La Sangre, but with my patients, out in the big bad world, being an atheist sure seems easier."

"Well, I get that part. If I'd listened to my father and not gone into the ministry, my life would have been easier. But what about the suffering, starvation in this world? And you hear all kinds of things in therapy, don't you? The addiction, the abuse. How does an atheist reconcile all that, seeing innocent children bearing the brunt of sick people? Look what Doyle went through, look how he's suffered, never happy, closed off from people."

"Well see, that's another place where atheism makes it easy. There isn't a cold, uncaring God who allows all that to happen. We don't have to cry out 'Why, God?' because there's no God to cry out to. We can just shrug and ascribe it to the folly of man."

"But then you just live and die."

"Yes, and when we're dead we won't know any differently, will we? No more suffering, no more pain. Hopefully we've done the best we could with our life, contributed something positive, but there's no more trying to get it perfect, no more hoping that things will get better, when they don't. No more believing and hoping in vain. They don't call death the final resting place for nothing."

Ralph didn't turn to Sal, he was too good a shrink for that. He watched the seagulls.

"I see your point," Sal finally said.

Ralph waited a moment. "It's been interesting though, as you and I have worked with Doyle, and getting to know each other. Sal, you and I do and say the exact same thing, except in a different vernacular. Where you say 'godly' or 'Christian' I say 'appropriate.' You say 'pray' and I say "examine yourself,' you say 'repent' and I say "take responsibility for your behavior.'" He tuned to Sal and raised his eyebrows in discovery. "Well, brother."

Hey Burt. Hey Roy. My wife asked me to complain to Nurse Walker about her husband always having his shirt off, especially when it's sunny. Did you? Yeah, I talked to Nurse Walker, and she said "Burt, I know when to tell my husband to put on a shirt, and if you don't like it you can take it up with the Pastor." Wow, Nurse Walker sure has changed since she married that carnival druggie. So are you going to talk to the Pastor? I don't know. I wish I could take *my* shirt off, but my wife won't let me. Yeah, mine won't either.

Maria and Bruno arrived at the Bodega Bay Lodge by noon, and she paid extra for the early check-in, glad the room was ready.

"Nice," Bruno commented when they entered the room.

"Yes," Maria replied, "I requested an ocean view."

But Bruno was looking at the king-sized bed, and Maria caught it.

"No Brutus, you just stay on your side, I'll

stay on mine. They didn't have a double room available with an ocean view. We have work to do, and I don't want you distracted."

Bruno didn't bother to correct the "Brutus" jab. He was working his way closer to Maria, he could even taste it. It was worth her occasional mild abuse.

Maria lay her suitcase on the bed and opened it, pulling out her bikini. "Come on, let's go for a swim."

"Are you kidding? You said you swam this morning, and besides the water is freezing up here!"

"Aw, don't be a sissy. And don't tell me you didn't bring your swim trunks!"

"Yeah, I brought my speedos, in case we use the hot tub."

"Speedos, right. That'll turn on the male staff at this place. Come on, get changed."

She started to undress and Bruno did the same, watching her.

By 2 PM, Corey was driving north on the Old Redwood Highway just out of Santa Rosa. On the left was the Journey's End Trailer Park, with the Indian hunched over his horse. A mile past it on the right was the yellow cinder-block building with the red sign, Adult Books, Private Video Booths. He pulled over and parked on the shoulder. He'd seen this building before, as a kid, but never thought about it one way or the other. Of course, that was before...well, *before*.

Although Corey's trailer was clearly identified as Lawrence Freeman Produce, he figured this one time, parked next to an adult book store for maybe 20 minutes, wouldn't hurt anything. Few people would notice, less would care. So see? Everything's all right. Just go in, get ten dollars worth of quarters, watch a few films, get his visual fix, and he's back on the road. Nothing wrong with that. The drop off was accepting Saturday delivery, so he'd actually be two days early. He'll call in for any pickups heading out of the Bay Area. Everything was in order.

He got change for his ten dollar bill at the counter and walked into the dark labyrinth of private booths.

"Hi Grace."

"Hi Connie! Always nice to hear from you!"

"I hate to be a pest..."

"Stop saying that!"

"Oh, well...I had another dream about Corey last night."

"Was it the one where Corey has black hair?"

"No, this was different. He looked normal, except for the long hair and kind-of beard, like you described him."

"Well, that's probably how you got that visual."

"I guess so, but this time he was wandering through a dark maze, black actually, narrow hallways with turns this way and that, and dead ends. Grace, I'm probably being a silly mother again, but as far as you know, he's all right?"

There was no way Grace could tell Connie that Corey had taken a route north to Eureka, which of course would take him right through Santa Rosa. "Yes, he is. In fact this last week that he stayed here, he didn't accept any jobs, and spent most of his time with me and my daughters and their families." Grace knew that Corey finding his own family in Bakersfield would hurt Connie, but she had to let Connie know that Corey was at least engaging with people. The grandchildren loved him.

"Oh," Connie managed. "I'm...glad. But I just can't shake that dream, it was so vivid. Grace, would it be okay with you if I was to say a prayer for Corey, and for you and me, right now on the phone?"

"Of course Connie! I'm afraid my prayers are limited to before meals and at church, but this will be good for me. Go right ahead, please."

Doyle slowly wandered through the black-painted narrow passageways, jiggling a handful of quarters like he was only there to look at videos, but also to give an understood signal to those interested. A kid was coming towards him, looking at the framed video covers on each booth, deciding which one he wanted. He was younger than Doyle preferred, but very good looking, blonde hair to his shoulders, a youthful, patchy beard.

"Got a ten," Doyle muttered when they approached each other.

"Oh well," the kid stopped, "they can give you change at the desk. I just changed a ten myself...." Corey looked into the man's face. "Doyle?"

SEVENTEEN

THE SECRET OF LA SANGRE

by Nathan Steer

The people of La Sangre live in a bubble that is fueled by enablement and symbiotic relationships. They are able, by mass hysteria, to create a world that is self-sustaining and inexplicably backward to everyone outside their bubble. Once within that bubble, the norm is redefined not as a majority or minority of people but as a communal view of the world outside. That view, founded in fear, is their normal.

The townspeople are euphorious and "happy," their religion works for them, and if no one else can understand it, who cares? After all, who can judge what happiness is? Maybe that was La Sangre's secret, they didn't exactly close themselves off to the rest of the world, they just made their own non-destructive rules. With proper self-governing, it seems they have successfully created, or re-created, the timeless concept of Utopia,

Lost Horizon, or Brigadoon. La Sangre is not new, and again, not overtly destructive.

Why then, do outsiders feel the need to tear it down?

"**B**ULLSHIT" Nathan screamed out. "IT'S ALL BULLSHIT!"

"Hey!" Julie came running in from the kitchen. "*What* is wrong? Take a break!"

"It's not working! Nothing's going to work! I CAN'T CRACK IT!"

"But...but it's just about the Santa Rosa Art Festival. You usually knock those out pretty quickly."

"It's not that," Nathan muttered to the keyboard.

Julie never read over his shoulder, she learned that back when they were dating, but she could see the title well enough on the screen, *The Secret Of La Sangre*. She sat down on the day bed, giving Nathan a few respectful seconds to come down to a manageable level. "Nathan, do you remember your conversation with Matthew in his den, after dinner with him and Lillian?"

"You mean where he questioned my motive for writing this book? What about it?"

Julie ignored his nasty tone. "You were put off..."

"*Pissed* off. Yeah, it was a hard question, I'll give him that, and I know the answer. My motive is to get published."

"Okay. So..." Julie searched for the words, holding her breath.

"So what?"

She exhaled. She had to be careful. "Nathan, you remember that Alfred Hitchcock seminar you took me to when we were dating? One of the speakers said that one of Hitchcock's skills was that he made the audience sympathize with the criminals, even Norman Bates in 'Psycho.' You felt for Norman Bates and understood why he had to kill. It was deplorable of course, but at least you understood why he did what he did." Should she take it further? Oh, too late now. "Maybe there needs to be more sympathy, more, well, *love* in your book."

"So you're saying I have to start loving a bunch of religious fanatics? There was a suicide/murder in that sick town, how can you find love in that?"

Julie sat and waited. When Nathan gave no response to his own question, she said "Lunch will be ready in 15 minutes. Crab salad sandwiches. You want me to bring yours in here?"

"No," Nathan softened his tone. "Let's eat outside."

"Relax Doyle," Corey insisted in the parking lot of the adult book store. "This happens a lot; one time I ran into a guy that also drives for LFP, he's married like most of them, they just want to watch some dirty movies every once in a while. It's a little embarrassing, but we just have the attitude of 'I didn't see you here and you didn't see me here,' okay? That's what you do, it's all right."

"Oh...I..."

"It's okay Doyle," Corey repeated, "you probably haven't even done this before, or you'd know the guy at the counter could change your ten. Forget it, okay? Yeah, I'm a little embarrassed too, but...." Corey looked around; he wanted to get out of here, and away from Doyle. There's no way he was going into La Sangre after this chance meeting. "I'm going to take off. Good to see you." He slapped Doyle on the shoulder and turned to leave.

"Where...where are you going?" Doyle asked him.

"I have a load to drop in Eureka."

"Can I...can I ride with you?"

"Aw Doyle, I can't take riders, you know that." Corey was getting the old Doyle-annoys-me feeling he'd always had. Doyle annoyed everyone in La Sangre; even those pious, holier-than-thou Christians couldn't hide what they felt about him.

"I just want to...talk to somebody," Doyle looked down.

Hey Corey, you just ran into Doyle in that place. Do you think you're any better than he is?

Who's being holier-than-thou now?

Corey's annoyance faded. "Hey Doyle...did have you have lunch yet? Sounds like you don't have any other plans."

"Yeah, I have the day off. I got a kid—little Tommy, you remember him—running the gas station. I might go spend some time with Matt and Lillian at the kiddieland in Codding Town. Sometimes I run the roller coaster while they take a lunch break. It's fun, you can assist me. They bring me lunch."

"Matthew? Oh, the guy she married, the one from Seattle. So he's still at that kiddieland, not back out on the road?"

"No, the kiddieland is doing real well, he's making good money. Do you...do you want to run over and see them, just to say hi? Lillian would like to see you. It's been a long time since you left."

Corey nodded. It had been a long time, almost a year. Lillian was always a good friend to Corey. She wasn't like his parents, she never lied to him. He'll never forget the dinner she cooked for him and Pete, their long conversation, Lillian telling them about her affair with Matthew in Seattle.

"Yeah," Corey said after a moment. "Yeah, let's do that. I have time. Tell you what, I'll park my rig at the Santa Rosa Truck Stop, you know where that is?"

Doyle nodded. He'd actually walked through it a few times at night, looking for men, and actually saw a Lawrence Freeman Produce truck there a few times. Just think, what if he had knocked on the driver door of one of those trucks and Corey opened it?

"So follow me there," Corey interrupted Doyle's what-if. "I'll check in and jump in your truck. All right?"

"All right."

Maria and Bruno had the outdoor jacuzzi at the Bodega Bay Lodge to themselves, so they were able to make their La Sangre plans there. Somehow it seemed more businesslike there than in the confines of their room, like a corporate or Mafia meeting.

"So what time will it be dark in La Sangre tonight?" Maria asked Bruno, who was watching her bikini restrained breasts float above the bubbling water line.

"I checked," he said. "Not til nine."

"That late?"

"It's June 15 today, the longest day of the year is June 21."

"Oh yeah. Well, we'll arrive at nine. Where are we going to park?"

"Shawn said that we could park in front of the General Store, it's on the south end of town, mostly hidden from everyone."

"Okay, I'll call Ruby and tell her."

"You're going to call? You never do that."

"I have no choice, I wanted to make sure we were situated here first. But I'll use the pay phone."

"Not the one in the lobby. Use the one at the gas station. The call to Ruby shouldn't be traced here."

"I *know* that, Brutus! The gas station, yes!"

Bruno held in. It was almost over. Just one more, and then they have the bed tonight. He'll finally be able to touch her. Maybe do even more, if she's ready. He'll be patient, but it's been so long that he's loved her from afar, he can't wait much longer.

"How about we walk over to The Tides for dinner?" Maria said. "I'll call Ruby then, she'll be waiting for my call. She should, I've paid that bitch over five hundred dollars."

Bruno just looked at her. That last comment, simple as it was, encapsulated Maria's relationships with people, himself included. Even after she'd shared her horrible childhood with him, he still doesn't *know* this woman. After a brief fantasy about what might happen in bed tonight and how long he's waited for it, it hit him. She's a blank slate.

"Hello? Bruno? Are you there?" Maria demanded.

"Uh...yeah. You'll call from the gas station."

"Yes, and then we'll have dinner at The Tides.

What's the matter with you? Are you *listening* to me?"

"Yes, I am, yes."

"I want lobster. Ruby sure talks about it enough, but how can it be any better than at the Santa Cruz Wharf? Lobster is lobster. She just orders lobster because it's the most expensive item on the menu. And it's also the only way she can get a date."

Bruno nodded, suddenly wanting to be anywhere else. Home, that was it. He wanted to be home...wherever that was, but it wasn't Maria's beach house.

A young couple in swim attire was coming toward the jacuzzi.

"Come on, let's go," Maria told him.

"Yes. Okay."

Doyle parked his pickup in the parking lot next to Codding Kids Town.

"This is new," Corey commented when they got out. It was indeed a kiddie park, not just some kiddie rides sitting haphazardly on pavement. It was wood-fenced with grass and shrubbery, and attractive game and food stands. There was a good crowd this Saturday, the rides were all operating at once with parents snapping photos of their kids in paradise.

Doyle and Corey walked over to the "Codding Coaster," where Matthew was manning the brake while Lillian was standing at the top of the entrance ramp, taking tickets and directing the line of kids into their seats. Doyle led Corey up the exit ramp.

"Matt, Lillian!" Doyle called. "Look who's here!"

They both looked up, Matthew with a blank look and Lillian slow on recognition. "Corey?" she called.

Corey nodded and followed Doyle onto the loading platform. "Hi Lillian."

"Hi! Hold on a second, let us get the train out." She walked along the coaster train, locking the restraints, then gave a thumbs-up to Matthew who released the brake and sent the coaster up the lift, the kids squealing in anticipation. Lillian went to Corey and gave him a hug. "Come over and meet Matthew, he has to stay next to the brake."

"Hi Matthew," Corey extended his hand.

"Call me Matt. I've heard a lot about you, Corey," Matthew greeted him with cautious warmth.

Corey waited until the screaming train ran through the station for its second time around. "I can imagine. I'm probably the talk of La Sangre."

Matthew held his hand out flat and wiggled it. "Eeeh."

Corey smirked. "That's what I figured."

"Well Corey!" Lillian lightened it up. "What

do you think of our roller coaster?"

"I rode this as a kid at the county fair."

"Well let me tell you, sonny," Matthew said, "this is the very same one. I bought it from some old-timer cheap, overhauled it, new brakes, re-upholstered the seats, new engine for the lift—that's how I got electrocuted," he glanced at Lillian, who slowly shook her head. "Okay hold on, we have to bring the train in and unload it. They just get two times around." He pulled on the station brake and the train came to a halt, the kids laughing and clapping. Lillian walked along the train and unlocked the restraints, pointed towards the exit, and then motioned for the kids anxiously waiting at the top of the en-trance ramp to come in and take their seats.

After the new train was sent out, Lillian asked "Doyle, do you mind stepping in for me? I want to talk to Corey for a few minutes."

"Sure!" Doyle enjoyed it. He knew all about the safe operation of the ride.

Lillian and Corey walked down the exit ramp and a short ways away from the noise of the coaster. "Oh, it's so good to see you, Corey. Does your mother know you're here? She didn't men-tion it to me."

"No, she doesn't know. I'm taking a load up to Eureka. I ran into Doyle, he told me you were here." He looked westward. "I don't know if I'll go into La Sangre."

Lillian gave a non-committal shrug, not wanting to push it. "I won't mention it to your mom."

Corey hesitated. "I just don't know how I feel about it, Lillian, especially staying at my parents' house. But Doyle told me that my room over the gas station is still available, he said he's kept it cleaned. Maybe I'll crash there tonight, I don't know, it might remind me of that one time..."

"Yes, I know what you mean. Do you have to leave right away?"

"I don't have to drop the load in Eureka until Monday."

"Well, you could surprise your parents for Father's Day. They'd like that."

"Father's Day," Corey repeated sardonically.

"I know Corey, I understand what you've been through, believe me. If you can rise above it, it would be a nice thing to do." She looked into his eyes. "And, I believe, it would be the *right* thing to do."

"Did my mother do the right thing?" Corey countered. "Keeping the truth about my father from me, and from Sal for that matter? And Sal, after admitting he was responsible for Pete's death? Was all that the 'right thing to do?'"

"I know Corey, your mother and I have talked about this. Sometimes we just do the wrong thing, we don't know any better." She looked over to where Matthew was operating the coaster. "I know I sure did, misjudging Matthew, hating him—all men—all these years when I'm the one who made the mistake. I told you and Peter that story at dinner. If I could turn back time I would, but I can't."

Corey absorbed her counsel, however begrudgingly. "I guess I understand that well enough, and yeah, I suppose I could see my mother, and Sal. But it's that whole town, all the lies, the hypocrisy, the judgment. I can imagine what they say about me, not that I care. But Lillian, that town, why do you stay there?"

Lillian shrugged. "It's where we belong, me and Matthew. The people can be annoying, sure. But maybe, just maybe, we're making a difference, making them see the larger picture, see people as who they are and where they're at, not as 'saved' or 'unsaved.' Matthew sure stands up to them, he doesn't take what calls their CBS."

"CBS?"

"Christian Bull Shit."

Corey chuckled. "I like that."

"Surprisingly, while they may not particularly like Matthew, they respect him. And in the meantime, your Dad's..."

"Sal."

"...your *stepfather's* sermons are wonderful now, positive and enlightening, practical and encouraging. He's really changed, Corey, I wish you'd give him another chance. Won't you stay? At least go to church tomorrow. I think you'll be glad you did."

"And then go to that ridiculous annual Father's Day picnic? Smile and shake hands and pretend I'm glad to be there?"

"No, no picnic this year."

"That's a first."

"I know. Sal told everyone just to celebrate it in their homes, have their own dinners. And Corey," Lillian looked at him, "you should meet your little brother."

("Get your ass home, Corey. And I don't mean Bakersfield!")

Corey looked away. "I don't know."

"Hi Ruby, it's Maria."

"Maria! It's just 3 o'clock! Are you in La Sangre already?"

"No, I'm calling from the pay phone at the gas station in Bodega Bay. We're checked into the Bodega Bay Lodge, and we'll come into La Sangre at nine, when it's dark. We're going to park in front of the General Store."

"Yeah, that's a good place. No one will notice your car there at night."

"So we'll just come to your house, right?"

"Yes. My house is the first one you come to when you walk down the road from the highway. It's painted a nice pink and green. From there we can figure out how you can meet up with Dr. Owen."

"Figure it out? You should already know how we're going to meet!"

"Oh but I do, I do! As we planned, his wife, Anne, is going to help us tonight with church cleaning for the Father's Day service tomorrow. I'll make sure she stays there, and then we'll walk over to the Owens' house. Maria, just what are you going to do with him?"

"Oh, I'm just going to talk to him about my sister Jessie."

"Well, I'm sure he'll be able to tell you everything you need to know. So, are you going to eat dinner at The Tides? The lobster is to die for!"

At Corey's request, he and Doyle took a drive south on the 101 to Mill Valley, then took Highway 1 through Muir Woods and met the ocean at Stinson Beach. They both took their shoes off and rolled up their jeans for a walk along the ocean.

"I didn't realize how much I missed the ocean until just now," Corey told him as they walked along the hard sand, the surf advancing and retreating, wetting their ankles and calves.

Doyle didn't respond. He was beginning to realize how much he enjoyed being with people now, with Matthew and Lillian, and now with Corey. It made that adult book store, the rest areas, the truck stops, all seem so...absurd. Jay had asked him "What are you looking for?" and

Sal had told him "We're your family."

They walked silently over a mile down the beach, then turned around.

"Hungry?" Corey asked Doyle.

"Yeah, I could eat something. There's that hamburger stand back on the One."

"Naw, let's get a real meal. How about The Tides, in Bodega Bay?"

"Oh, I can't afford that."

"It's on me, buddy."

"Oh no..."

"Doyle, I make a ton of money driving, I want to take you to dinner at The Tides. And you're going to order anything you want."

Doyle hesitated. "Lobster?"

"Lobster it is."

It was a somber Saturday at the Steer home, ever since Nathan's outburst that morning. He told Julie he was going out to do some yard work, but when she looked out the window while housecleaning he was just sitting on a lawn chair, shirtless, sunning himself. Well that's good, she thought, he always says how the sun recharges his creative batteries. He would often tell her, "I'm going to soak up some rays and then do some writing." But today he didn't come back inside.

Towards 5 PM she opened the back door. "Hon, I'm going to drive down to the butchers, get a couple of steaks, okay?"

He looked up. "No, let me go. I'll walk."

"Oh...okay."

"Rib eyes?"

"Yes. Do you feel like barbecuing?"

"Naw, just broil 'em." He got up, grabbed his shirt, went past her through the back door, and didn't pat her behind.

After he left, Julie wondered if she did the right thing, questioning his motive for writing the book. Oh well girl, the bell can't be unrung.

Nathan walked the mile to the specialty butcher, thinking that if the walk didn't settle any turmoil, at least the steaks will have reached room temperature by the time he got home. He might stop at the Fairgrounds Bar for a drink. After his talk with Matthew, instead of beer he'd switched to a single shot of Jack Daniels, with a Coke back.

Corey and Doyle waited at The Tides bar for a window seat, both drinking ginger ale. Thankfully the bartender didn't ask Corey for his ID to sit at the bar. Corey still had a couple years before he turned 21, but he didn't care. Legal drinking wasn't on his life's agenda, whatever that agenda was, but he was beginning to suspect that just driving a truck and making money wouldn't be enough.

They didn't talk, and they were both

comfortable with it. At one point Corey caught Doyle watching someone with interest through the mirror behind the bar. Corey followed his gaze and saw a huge, overbuilt man, obnoxiously wearing a tank top, seated at a nearby table. Wait, he looks familiar. Corey made a casual turnaround on his bar stool as if scanning the room. Oh yeah, he knew that muscle-head with no neck, but from where? Fortunately the man didn't notice Corey looking at him, engrossed as he was with the woman across from him. All Corey saw of her from the back was long, flowing, dark brown hair. ("Here Corey," Sabrina threw the dark brown wig at him. "I don't think I'll be needing this anymore.")

Maria. With her Brutus.

Corey turned back to the bar. Maria. This was way too much happening in one day. God was really laying some shit on him: the Journey's End sign, running into Doyle at the adult book store, getting lectured by Lillian, and now this. And today is exactly a year after Pete Freeman came into town, the day before Father's Day. Corey had an impulse to bolt from the restaurant, have Doyle drive him back to his truck, and drive north on the 101 to Eureka. ("Get your ass home, Corey. And I don't mean Bakersfield!")

"I hate Father's Day," Corey declared.

"Me too."

The steak was marbled, tender and juicy, the baked potatoes crisp on the outside, soft inside, with the green beans and salad both fresh and well seasoned. At Julie's request, Nathan opened a bottle of their most expensive red wine.

"This is better than eating at The Tides," Julie attempted dinner conversation.

"Yeah babe," Nathan responded politely. "Real good. Thank you."

This writer's block was different from Nathan's usual ones, Julie deduced. It was more like depression, not just a mood that Nathan usually went into and out of relatively quickly. She'd been wondering when to bring something up that was nagging her, but now wasn't the time.

Or maybe it was. Maybe Nathan needs to think about something else than just his writing. "Nathan," she threw caution to the wind, "what would you think if we were to stop using the diaphragm?"

Nathan looked up at her and answered in a flat tone. "Sure. Fine. Tomorrow *is* Father's Day, isn't it?"

Julie didn't respond to the punch. She had it coming. She saw his mood, she should have just let him be.

After dinner they sat outside and finished off the bottle of wine, which gave them both a warm buzz.

"You know what I'd like to do right now?" he

said, looking at the setting sun.

"What?" she asked hopefully.

"Watch 'The Birds.'"

Oh no, not "The Birds" again. Since they bought the Betamax machine, Nathan was building up quite a tape library, including most of Alfred Hitchcock's films. Besides, he still had to write the article on the Santa Rosa Art Festival for submission in the morning. "Sure Hon, that would be nice."

"Hi Connie, it's Grace."

"Oh Grace, thank you for calling." Connie was conscious of them always talking about her own needs, not enough about Grace's. "How are you?"

"Oh, okay I guess. I suspect the Father's Day thing has me down. It's been a year since..." her voice cracked.

"Oh Grace, I'm sorry."

"Well," Grace cleared her throat, "all four girls and their families will be here tomorrow, their husbands are all fathers now. I'm glad that they use my home for their celebrations. We did last Christmas here."

"Oh, that's nice." Connie debated before asking, "Will Corey be there?"

"No Honey, he had a load to take, he's driving over the weekend."

"Oh."

He'll be driving right by your home, Grace thought sadly. Poor thing. "Connie, how's everything there?"

"Sad, in a way, about Father's Day like you say. Of course," Connie checked to make sure Sal was out of hearing, and lowered her voice, "this time it's a real Father's Day for Sal, this time his very own boy. But still, he announced there'd be no Father's Day picnic like usual."

"Maybe that's better. Connie, I have a funny feeling, but I don't know what it is."

"Did you have a dream?"

"If I did, nothing I could decipher. You?"

"No, no dream. But Grace, I have a strange feeling too, about tomorrow, even about tonight. There's nothing I can tell you, but...I'll get through this weekend easier if we can make plans to talk, say Sunday night? 9 PM okay?"

"That would be perfect for me, everyone will be gone by then. I hired a cook to handle the meal, and she'll do all the cleanup."

"So okay then, Grace. I'll talk to you then."

"Okay sweetie. And try not to worry, okay?"

"I'll try. I love you Grace."

"I love you Connie."

Julie and Nathan sat on the couch, his arm around her, and enjoyed the film's familiar locale, including one aerial shot of Tippi Hedren driving north into Bodega Bay, in which, if you knew where to look, you could for a split second see the small blob of buildings that is La Sangre, in the top left corner of the screen.

Julie fell asleep halfway through the movie, aided by the wine, while Nathan remained engrossed as usual up to the frighteningly ambiguous ending. He always loved the ending, with the main characters slowing driving their car through a field of immobile, resentful birds that could turn to anger and attack at the slightest provocation.

But this time the ending affected Nathan differently. The suspense was still there, but for the first time he saw, in his mind, an epilogue after the film ended. He didn't know where it came from, but he knew it was true.

"Tonight!" he cried out in hellish premonition. "The birds are attacking tonight!"

Julie jolted awake. "What? What Nathan, what?"

EIGHTEEN

Corey was determined not to leave The Tides. He won't cower for Maria, not for anyone. She and her Brutus left their table while Corey and Doyle were still at the bar, passing close enough for Corey to hear Maria say something about "those damn seagulls" while Bruno dutifully and stupidly replied "yeah."

Since those two days at Waddell Beach, Corey could remember every detail of the sex, but nothing about the woman herself. He now knew that if he was trying to recreate their one-off encounter with all his trysts out on the road, it was fantasy based on unreality; the center couldn't hold. Maybe there was something to those SAA meetings.

After dinner—lobster for both of them—they walked out to the end of the Bodega Bay wharf. The sun had just set, the sky an unusual burnt orange.

"Doyle," Corey said as they were leaning against the rail, "I think I do want to go back to La Sangre, stay in my room over the gas station.

Has it changed?"

"Your room?"

"No, the town, the people, the way of life there."

Doyle shrugged. "La Sangre is still La Sangre. Foggy...and blurry."

Just like Corey's life has been for the last ten months, with La Sangre following him all over the country like an angry ghost, a ghost that Corey fought with his drug of choice. "I need to see it, knowing what I know now," he told Doyle. "But I'm not ready to see my parents. Maybe tomorrow morning."

"Tell you what. The gas station's closed by now. I'll pull behind the pumps and you can sneak up the stairs to your room."

"I don't know, that seems kind of cowardly."

"I know what you mean Corey. I'm not sure I want to live there any more. I've realized that everyone in La Sangre has been laughing at me."

"I was one of them," Corey turned to him. "I'm sorry Doyle."

"Forget it kid." Doyle gave a faint smile. "Maybe I'd better take another meeting with Dr. Owen."

"Dr. Owen? The psychiatrist?"

"I think it's helping."

"Maybe I ought to see him too."

Doyle shrugged. "Can't hurt. He puts things

together for me, better than your...the Pastor can."

"Look, there's the General Store," Maria pointed to the first building on the left.

Bruno pulled over and parked in front of it. "You don't get up here, do you?" he observed.

"No. Jessie always drove down to me. But I've driven through here before, it gives me the creeps. Once I stopped at that so-called Last Chance Gas Station," she pointed to it, "there was a weirdo running it, a tall, skinny old guy who was really," she wrinkled her nose, "bitter."

"You could relate to him?" It came out of Bruno's mouth unexpectedly.

"So who suddenly died and made you a psychiatrist, Dr. Brutus?"

Bruno shut up; it was a game of chess with her. With the right moves on his part, including when to keep his mouth shut, Maria could start to love him. He wanted to believe his momentary piercing of her armor got his knight one square closer to her queen. It occurred to him that Maria didn't know what a good chess player he was. Those old chess players on the Santa Cruz Wharf thought he was stupid because of how he looked, until he captured their queen within thirty minutes. He often wondered if he should go pro.

"Let's wait until it gets completely dark,"

Maria decided. "Another ten minutes."

"Okay."

Corey hit the bed at 9 PM. After his comfort-able sleeping accommodations in his truck and in his father's bed, he hated the sagging mat-tress in this room above the gas station, but he was too beat to care. The room was never used until Corey moved in after his home-schooled graduation a year ago, but he'd only slept here that one night, with Pete Freeman in the other worn out bed.

As Corey passed into a restless slumber, he knew that he would never finish the night here.

When all the ladies, including Anne Owen, were finished cleaning up and decorating the church for Father's Day, Ruby took a moment at 9 PM to go out the church door and look south. Sure enough, there was the gold BMW that Maria had described. In fact, two figures, a tall female, probably Maria, and a huge male were just getting out of the car. Ruby said good night to the ladies leaving the church, but stopped Anne and asked if she would help her in the church kitchen, it really needs some scrubbing, would she mind?

"Okay, let's go," Maria told Bruno as he made sure all the car doors were locked. They began walking north to the dirt road leading down to the homes. "Ruby's house is the first one we'll come to, pink and green."

Bruno could have said "Yeah, I know, Shawn told me that," but Maria's always-short fuse was at its end, ready for the final big explosion. She should have just stayed at the car and let him do it, but no, she wanted to watch. Like she had watched him with her father in the ocean.

"Come on, Brutus! Step it up a little!"

Maria was ravenous; she could smell the blood of La Sangre.

The church kitchen was already spotless and didn't need cleaning. Anne would have told Ruby so, not to mention her humiliation as a char-woman. But she realized that this time alone with Ruby—a first—could crack open *The Secret of La Sangre*. Ruby *knew* something, Anne was certain of that. She didn't know what it was, but Ruby had been obviously dodging her all this time. Now, with the two of them alone, Anne will get Ruby talking. She'll show her husband what a good journalist she is. She only wished she'd remembered to bring the mini-cassette recorder.

"What's in there?" Anne pointed to a closed door next to the refrigerator.

"Oh, we won't go in there. That's storage; Christmas decorations, stuff like that. The Pastor has some things in there, file cabinets, stuff he doesn't need in his office."

Files? Anne wondered. About what, members of the congregation? About Jessie? Maybe nothing, but no stone goes unturned. This was better than getting Ruby talking, she can always do that.

"Anne, I'm going to run home for my Playtex gloves, the ones here are dirty. Do you want me to bring you a pair?"

"Oh, please," Anne nodded, trying to appear nonchalant. This will give her a few minutes to rummage through the Pastor's file cabinets. She grabbed a sponge and rinsed it under the tap. "I'll go ahead and get started."

"Okay Honey," Ruby said brightly, "I'll be right back!"

"Okay!" Anne matched Ruby's tone. As soon as Ruby was out the back door, Anne went into the storage room and shut the door.

Ruby hurried out of the church and intercepted Maria and the huge man at the dirt road.

"Maria?" Ruby squealed, and rushed into a full hug.

"Quiet Ruby!" Maria pushed her back, disgusted. God, this lady *is* crazy. Are all Christians like this?

"Come on down to the house!" Ruby giggled softly, not noticing the rebuff. "It's right over there!"

Maria and Bruno followed Ruby, who suddenly stopped.

"Wait a minute," Ruby pointed to a man's moonlit figure at the cliff. "That's him. That's Dr. Owen!"

"Are you sure?" Maria asked. "I don't want the wrong person, now."

"Yes, that's him. He's been doing a lot of that lately at night, especially around full-moon time."

"Bruno." Maria's command was clear and simple.

Bruno was on it. It was moments like this, when Maria let him take charge, that he moved his knight forward on the chess board that was their relationship. He took hold of Maria's left arm to steer her toward the figure at the cliff. "Come on, Maria, we're going to talk to him first, just like we said." She yanked her arm away. He ignored it and turned back to Ruby. "You can go home now, Miss. Thank you."

It was clearly an order not to be disobeyed. Ruby, confused, looked back at the church, wondering about Mrs. Owen, who was in there scrubbing away. But she'd better do what this monster said. After all, he knew her name. She went home, suddenly deathly afraid.

Ralph heard the tromping of grass approaching from behind him, and turned around. The

eastern moon could only backlight the two figures walking towards him with a purpose, but
the feeling was unmistakable: hostility. Years
of therapy sessions gave him a built-in hostility
meter. This time it had jumped to the red.

"Dr. Owen, do you know me?" the woman
spoke in attack mode.

"No," Ralph remained steady. "Should I?"

"You know my sister, Jessie Malana." She
stopped ten feet away from him, not wanting to
get any closer to him than she had to. Bruno was
at her side.

"Jessie?" Ralph's fear spiked. "Why, what..."

"Don't try to dance with me, you Christian
shrink!" Maria raised her voice.

"But I'm not a...."

"You took advantage of her vulnerability, her
pain, AND YOU FUCKED HER!"

"What? I did no such thing!"

"YOU DON'T DO THAT TO CHILDREN!"
Bruno took Maria's rage inside himself.   He
had his purpose, his goal.   No pain no gain.
"YOU DON'T DO THAT TO CHILDREN!" he
screamed again.

Ruby was grabbing two sets of Playtex gloves
when she heard the shouting and looked out
the kitchen window. In the moonlight she saw
someone—Pastor Satori!—walking towards Dr.
Owen, Maria, and the monster. Oh God! What

did I start? What have I done?

As Sal approached ("Run and jump Sal!") all three of them turned.

"Ralph?" Sal asked the obviously frightened man.

"Sal, they...she's accusing me of having sex with Jessie Malana!"

"Oh God..." Sal choked.

"She must be the one," Ralph pointed at the woman, "who filed that complaint against me."

"You're goddamned right I did, with the California Psychiatric Assholes, and they took your fucking side! THEY TOOK YOUR FUCKING SIDE! THEY ALWAYS DO! DON'T THEY?"

"Miss..." Sal made an attempt.

"MISS MALANA, JESSIE'S SISTER! AND YOU'RE THAT BASTARD OF A PASTOR, WHO FILLED MY SISTER UP WITH ALL YOUR CHRISTIAN BULLSHIT, AND BETWEEN YOU AND THIS SHRINK, YOU DESTROYED HER!"

"But Miss Malana, it wasn't Ralph who had sex with your sister, it was..."

"DON'T DEFEND HIM! YOU MEN ALWAYS HUDDLE UP TOGETHER, DON'T YOU! THIS FUCKING SHRINK KNEW THAT SEX MADE MY SISTER GO CRAZY, BUT HE TOOK HER ANYWAY! HE RAPED HER!" She turned her fury back to Ralph. "THAT'S WHY

SHE CRASHED HER CAR AT THE CLIFF! SHE KNEW YOU WERE GOING TO TRY TO FUCK HER AGAIN, IN YOUR OWN HOME! DID YOU LET YOUR WIFE WATCH WHEN YOU FUCKED HER IN REDDING? IS THAT THE ONLY SEX YOUR WIFE CAN GET, BY WATCHING?"

"YOU DON'T DO THAT TO CHILDREN!" Bruno roared, moving towards Ralph.

Ralph couldn't see the brute's eyes, but he knew instinctively his pupils were dilated.

Bruno was both focused and out of control, seeing only Dr. Owen, the enemy who had killed Jessie. Maria would at last love him for this.

It was the third "YOU DON'T DO THAT TO CHILDREN!" that told Ruby what was going to happen, what had been happening all along and she had been a part of it, titillated by the intrigue, the secret letters, men taking her for lobster dinner at The Tides, the checks from this woman who is...oh God, what have I been doing? She rushed from the window to the phone in her bedroom and dialed 9-1-1. "Oh God, please hurry! I'm so sorry!"

"Nine-one-one operator, what is your emergency?"

Ralph was standing with his back to the cliff, vulnerable, and the giant's first two threatening steps toward him became a maniacal lunge. Sal knew that as solid as he himself was, he'd bounce right off the monster. He knew what he had to do, just like Peter Freeman had done for Corey.

Run and jump Sal.

It took just one very long second.

He threw his body against Ralph's hip, knocking him down.

Sal took the hit.

In the church storage room, Anne heard the shouting outside near the cliff, but the crazy Christians often gathered there on fogless moonlit nights to shout praises to the Lord. It had scared her when she first heard it years ago, now she was used to it and kept rummaging. There must be *something* in here.

"BRUNO, WHAT THE FUCK DID YOU DO! YOU KILLED THE WRONG FUCKING ONE!"

"Well Maria, he just kind of got in front...."

Ralph had jumped up and was running on the dirt road up to Highway 1, not knowing where he was going, just anywhere away from the cliff, from the lunatic who just killed his best friend.

"GO AFTER HIM BRUTUS!" Maria shrieked. "HE'S A WITNESS! GET HIM!"

Always one more. Bruno finally knew his

ultimate truth. Always one more. He ran after the panicked man, who was running toward... what, the church? Does that fool really think he'll be protected in there? Some magic shield that'll prevent Bruno from doing his job? These fucking Christians *are* crazy, just like Maria said. She was right. She was always right. But he had only one more to go, and then she would let him love her, and she would love him.

Ralph got to the church, already winded, heard Bruno's satanic scream of "ALWAYS ONE MORE!" behind him. Like a miracle, screeching tires brought the familiar orange 1970 Plymouth Barracuda to a dime-stop next to him. Ralph grabbed the handle of the passenger door—unlocked, thank you God—jumped in and elbowed the door lock down, seconds before Bruno grabbed the handle, then slammed his fist on the passenger window.

"Ralph!" Matthew cried. "What the *hell* is going on?"

His question was answered by a THUD and the Incredible Hulk was on the hood of his car, beating on the windshield, lost in his insanity.

"He wants to kill me!" Ralph cried.

"I can see that! Fasten your seat belt!"

"What?"

"Put on your seat belt! I'm gonna give this crazy fool the carnival ride of his life!"

Matthew shoved the floor shift into first gear

and popped the clutch; the rear tires howled as they clawed for traction and the car lurched forward.

"ALWAYS ONE MORE!" Bruno screamed from the hood, grabbing hold of the cowl with both hands.

"He's insane!" Ralph cried.

"I can see that too!"

With his 440 CI Six Pack, it took Matthew just five seconds to tear southward through town, zig-zagging to dislodge the hood ornament from hell, which showed no fear, just blind determination, repeating "ALWAYS ONE MORE!"

"I can't lose him Ralph! Are you buckled up?"

Bruno beat the windshield with his right fist.

"Yes!" Ralph cried. "What are you going to..."

Bruno switched hands and tore off the left windshield wiper.

"Hold on!"

Matthew hit the brakes at the right moment that would give his prized Barracuda minimal damage—so he hoped—and get rid of something that reeked of pure evil.

"ALWAYS ONE MORE!" Bruno screamed for the last time as the Barracuda hit the guard rail at the turn. The cowl snapped off in his hands and he flew backwards over the rail and down to the ocean.

Bruno thought he would be hitting the rocks but instead fell into blackness, landing on his feet on a workout treadmill that was going so fast he was thrown backwards and fell further through the blackness onto another treadmill. This time Bruno began to run the treadmill to avoid another slip backward through blackness.

So he ran on the treadmill, while an invisible discordant choir sang *"ALWAYS ONE MORE! ALWAYS ONE MORE! ALWAYS ONE MORE!"*

He ran.

Always one more.

He knew these machines, he lived these machines. They had created him.

Always one more.

He ran.

Always one more.

His arms pumped furiously, his feet pounding, his thighs and the backs of his calves screaming, his lungs exploding.

Always one more. No pain, no gain.

For Eternity.

NINETEEN

"Corey!" Doyle banged on his door across the hall. "COREY!"

Corey opened the door, pulling up his jeans. "Yeah Doyle, I heard the siren, I thought I was dreaming. What's going on?"

"I don't know. I heard screaming a while ago, but I thought people were praying at the cliff. But now it sounds like the sheriff's siren. Come on!"

Corey put his running shoes on without socks, didn't bother to tie them, and they ran down the stairs and across the highway, neither of them noticing a beautiful insane woman over at the General Store, trying to break into a locked BMW.

Matthew's chest was bruised, his lower stomach creased from the seat belt. He felt around his body, he was all right. He looked over at Ralph.

"NO! I DIDN'T DO IT!" Ralph screamed. "I NEVER TOUCHED HER!"

Just what I need right now, a crazy shrink.

"Ralph, listen to me!" Matthew violently shook Ralph's left shoulder. "Look at me!" But Ralph just kept screaming.

Matthew got out of the car—at least the doors still worked—and went around the rear to the passenger door and opened it. He unfastened Ralph's seat belt and put his hands on Ralph's shoulders.

"Ralph! Look at me! Just *look* at me!"

"He flew over the cliff just like Jessie did! But I never laid a hand on her!"

"Come on Ralph, we have to get out!"

But Ralph couldn't be budged. He was in shock, Matthew knew that much. Lilly would likely have confirmed it. "Ralph," Matthew tried to be calm, "my car's not drivable, I'm sure the front end's pushed against the tires. We've got to get back to our homes, find out if our wives are all right! We can't stay here!" Matthew almost threw out his lower back trying to pull Ralph out of the vehicle.

"No!" Ralph continued to cry. "He died for me!"

"Yeah buddy, Jesus died for you, I'm on board with that, so what? Come on, we've got to..."

"No, no, not Jesus!"

"You don't mean that gorilla that just flew off my car! *He* died for you?"

"No! Sal! *Sal* died for me!"

"What are you talking about?" Matthew could see that Ralph was mentally gone, brute force wouldn't work, and Matthew couldn't leave him here alone either. Who knows what he might do? One body over the cliff was enough for one night. He looked at his watch, deciding to give it ten minutes for Ralph to calm down, before trying to get the big fellow out of the car and guide him back to town. Maybe they could get just as far as the gas station so he could use the pay phone to call 9-1-1. Most likely somebody already has.

Ruby was hiding, shaking, on the floor. squeezed between the wall and her bed. She'd called 9-1-1, that was enough. She stupidly gave her real name to the operator when asked, and then said "I think someone is being killed at the cliff in La Sangre," and hung up. There was nothing more that could be said. So she hid in her bedroom with the light off, not wanting God to see her, not wanting Him to know what she had put into motion, for money and a lobster dinner.

Matthew was annoyed and getting angry. Usually Lilly did this touchy-feely stuff. But he remained crouched alongside Ralph, who was still sitting in the passenger seat, immobile. Other than an occasional "He died for me!" he was uncommunicative. Matthew didn't dare leave him.

In the meantime, he was listening to the sirens; it sounded like one was the cops and the second one an ambulance, and then ten minutes later...was that a helicopter? Is Lilly all right? What the *hell* is going on? He could yell as loud as he wanted, but he knew no one could hear him this far away and over all the noise.

"You're really bugging me, Dr. Owen! You're the shrink, I should be the one cracking up and *you* taking care of *me*! Come on Buddy!" Matthew slapped him hard across the cheek. "LOOK AT ME!"

Ralph finally turned to Matthew. An acknowledgment at last.

"He died for me," he told Matthew sadly.

Maria had run after Bruno as he chased Dr. Owen up to Highway 1, then saw him leap onto an orange car like a wild animal, and take a joy ride down Highway 1 while screaming something stupid about "always one more!" Then she heard a thud further down the road.

She ran to her car parked at the General Store. It was locked. Bruno had driven, Bruno had the keys.

So Bruno let her down too. They always do. But the problem now was how will she get away without car keys? Maybe she could flag a car for a ride, but how likely is a car going to be traveling on this stretch of Highway One at night?

So she waited in the shadows of the General Store, away from the light of the moon, and thought, and planned. Nobody knew her here, she could cut her hair, bleach it, nobody could identify her.

Except Ruby. Ruby knew who she was. Ruby had even hugged her. Maybe that's what Bruno meant: always one more. Ruby was next.

So Maria waited and waited for a car, while hearing sirens and a helicopter arrive. She could even hear the townspeople shouting "Oh Jesus! Oh Jesus!"

Finally she saw someone walking from the south. Bruno? He would have the car keys, and they could drive away from this insane place. Maybe he hadn't let her down; he could have easily killed both the shrink and whoever was driving the car, and maybe he did. He really was the Incredible Hulk!

But no, it was two people. Walking slowly by was Dr. Owen, being half-held up by some tall thin guy. The gas station attendant? No, it was someone else, better looking. "You all right walking, Ralph?" he asked. Dr. Owen nodded and they continued slowly up the road. Maria waited until they turned down the dirt road to the homes, then moved back to the roadside, praying that a car would come by.

Nathan stayed at the cliff with his camera while the deputies marked off recent footprints in the grass, and he took photos per their direction. Julie was inside the Satori house with Lillian, Mrs. Owen, Corey, and Doyle. Connie was in the love seat with Lillian next to her. Corey was on the couch holding his little brother and Doyle sat next to them. He thought about leading the group in a prayer, but how would he pray? For Pastor Satori? For Dr. Owen? Not knowing who was at the bottom of the cliff, it would be a losing prayer either way. Still, Doyle began a silent prayer.

The front door burst open. Matthew and a recovering Ralph stumbled in.

Anne jumped up from her chair and ran to embrace him. "RALPH! ARE YOU ALL RIGHT? WHAT HAPPENED?" He placed a feebled arm around her and looked past her to Connie.

"Connie," he said shakily. "Sal..."

"Oh no!" Anne suddenly realized. She turned back to Connie, whose face was losing its color as she tried to stand up.

"No, sit Connie," Lillian gently ordered her, holding her down and keeping her arm around her shoulders.

Ralph gently broke from Anne's hold and took a few steps towards Connie. "I'm so sorry Connie, I saw it all. Sal is dead."

"NOOOO!" Connie screamed, struggling to

get up as Julie helped Lillian hold her firmly. "We had a fight! I said some horrible things I didn't mean...oh God...Sal, I didn't mean it! I love you, I didn't mean it!"

"Sal knows you love him, Connie," Matthew said gently. "He knows."

Lillian checked Connie's pulse and looked into her eyes. She nodded okay to Ralph. Julie went into the kitchen for a cold cloth.

"But...but how did it happen?" Connie cried. "Why?"

"There was a crazy man," Matthew said, maintaining a calm tone, "from out of town. Somehow," he looked at Ralph, who nodded approval for Matthew to continue, "well, he got in a fight with Sal and shoved him off the cliff. The crazy man was caught." There was no point going into detail, not yet. "I'm so sorry Connie. There was nothing Sal or anyone else could have done."

Matthew whispered to Ralph and then addressed the group. "Ralph and I have to tell the sheriff what happened, what we saw. We'll explain more after we talk to him." He went over to Lillian and gave her a kiss on the cheek, she nodded at him, then he and Ralph went out.

"Mom!" Corey suddenly cried out, looking over at his mother. "I'm so sorry!" He got up carefully with baby Freeman and went over to her. Lillian took the baby and Corey sat down next to his mother, putting his arm around her.

"Oh Corey," Connie sobbed into his shoulder, "I'm so glad you're home!"

Lillian gently placed Freeman Satori in Connie's arms, and he gave a joyful infant's cry.

Maria heard a vehicle coming, heading southward. At last! She made herself visible at the edge of the road and a red Ford F-250 pickup stopped beside her. The driver leaned over and opened the passenger door.

She looked inside. "You!"

"Yes, we met before, Maria," Jay nodded. "one night on the beach, at your house, you'd just come in from swimming. Remember? We talked."

"Yes...yes, I remember. I was naked, but you looked into my eyes."

"Do you want a lift?"

Maria didn't hesitate. For the first time since she was a child she climbed into a vehicle driven by a man and wasn't afraid. She shut the door and found the seat belt, but then looked at him. "Do you mind...is it all right if I sit next to you?"

"Of course. There's a seat belt here," he patted the middle of the bench seat.

After she was buckled up, Jay drove the truck south, with Maria hiding her face against his shoulder as they passed the orange muscle car rammed against the guard rail.

"He's dead?" Maria asked. "Bruno?"

"Yes, he's dead."

"I need to talk. Will you listen to me? Like you did that night on the beach?"

"Yes Maria, I'll always listen to you."

"That night, at the beach, you understood what I went through."

"I did understand, and I should know. I suffered it myself."

"You did?"

Jay nodded. "A long time ago."

"What am I going to do? Will you help me?"

"Of course I will. What I'll do is drive you to Bodega Bay, that's as far as I'll take you. There's a pay phone at the gas station, the one you used earlier today. You're going to dial 9-1-1, you don't need a coin for that."

"You're going to leave me there?"

"I'll never leave you Maria. But I'll send you the best defense lawyer to handle your case."

"Where will you be?"

"Standing next to you in court."

"But why couldn't you help me before? Why couldn't you stop it?"

"I can't, Maria, not when there's free choice. Innocent people, children, get hurt as a result. But there's hope."

"Hope?"

"I can't obliterate sin from the Earth, not quite yet. But in the meantime you'll be able to help so many women who have suffered this. They'll know that you'll listen to them, and that you understand what they've been through."

"Where will I do this, in prison?"

"We'll see, Maria. But wherever it is, I'll be with you."

After Dr. Owen and Matthew told Sheriff Daley what had happened, the three of them got into the sheriff's car and drove to the hairpin turn. "So Sheriff," Matthew asked him dryly in the car, "what am I looking at here, manslaughter?"

"I think you'll do fine with self-defense, Mr. Grant, with a psychiatrist as a witness no less."

"Good. I'm just wondering what my insurance company will think."

"I'm writing it up as assault and vandalism."

"Cool. It'll be a comp claim, won't raise my premium."

Ralph appreciated Matthew's levity. It was a tool he often used in therapy. Humor and laughter was cleansing, it followed tears.

The sheriff parked behind Matthew's Barracuda; they got and looked down the cliff with the sheriff's spotlight. The body was lying face up on the rocks; even at 70 feet the spotlight caught its wide-open eyes, and wide-open mouth. A wave washed over it. After a few moments Ralph turned away and sat on the guard rail for more regrouping, while Matthew examined his poor orange 'Cuda. The grill was smashed and all the coolant lost, the front fender was indeed lodged against the tires, the hood popped open. But the engine block seemed fine, no oil was leaking. "Thank you Jesus!" he shouted.

"Mr. Grant," Daley said after he was satisfied with what he could see with his spotlight, "would you mind going to get Nathan? I need him to snap some photos. I should have thought of that and brung him along. I'll stay here."

"Sure Sheriff, and it's Matt. Mind if I take your car? Mine's out of commission."

Daley chuckled. "Sure, take my car, and have Nathan drive it back. You two are through for a while, better tend to your wives."

A helicopter approached, with KLS-TV illuminated on the sides. "Yep, here come the San Francisco stations," Daley shook his head. Just what he needed. Where do they think they're going to land? Well, his deputies knew how to deal with those vultures.

The chopper's noise was joined by the siren of yet another rescue vehicle approaching La Sangre. "Well that's good," Daley sighed, "they have two bodies to deal with now."

"Just like last year," Dr. Owen said.

He and Sheriff Daley regarded each other for a moment, then shook their heads.

When Matthew and Ralph stepped into the Satori home, there was some semblance of order. In the kitchen Mrs. Owen was making more coffee and scrounging for cookies, crackers, cheese, anything she could put out. Connie was still holding her baby on the love seat with Corey beside her and Lillian sitting vigilante nearby. Julie had left to join Nathan, and Doyle left to see if the deputies needed any help. Dr. Owen checked Connie out and suggested a mild sedative, but she shook her head.

Matthew leaned over and whispered to Corey, "Can you come outside for a minute?"

Corey looked at him, then turned to his mother and said "I'll be right back."

Connie nodded.

"Man talk," Matthew said to her, placing his hand gently on her cheek.

Outside it had quieted down. The rescue chopper was gone, the team determining it was more expedient and safer to use a winch and repel down the cliff and retrieve the body. The deputies had chased off the news chopper. Corey and Matthew watched for a minute from the deck.

"So what do you want to tell me?" Corey asked Matthew. "Not another body?"

"Well...yes. The guy that killed your father was found, he's dead."

"Police shot him?"

Matthew hesitated, there was no point in describing how it happened, not yet anyway. "No, he's at the bottom of the cliff, down at the turn."

"What? Where Jessie...?"

Matthew nodded tiredly. "But right now I'm thinking of something else." He put his hands on Corey's shoulders, the boy looking older than the one he'd called "sonny" earlier that day. "Tomorrow at church..."

"Church?"

"Yes, church. You're going to give the sermon."

"WHAT? Are you crazy? After all this, you're talking about *church*? Are you talking CBS?"

Matthew had to chuckle; Lilly had told him about her conversation with Corey. "No, I don't think so, but tomorrow, you'll deliver the sermon...."

"Are you insane? That *is* CBS! I can't do that!"

"You can, Corey, and you will. Believe me, you'll be doing it more for yourself than for Sal. And you'll be doing it for your mother, that you have so cruelly ignored this last year. Stop thinking about yourself for a change and start thinking about her. *And* your little brother."

The last punch hit Corey in the gut.

"Yes," Matthew softened his tone and took his hands from Corey's shoulders. "Your little brother, Freeman. Now for your sermon, let's see, what was your father's favorite scripture?"

Corey shook his head. "Uh...after my Dad, Pete, died...I guess John 15:13."

"Which one is that?"

"'Greater love has no man than this, than he lay down his life for his friends,'" said Jay coming up the deck stairs, Barney at his side.

Corey and Matthew turned to him.

"Well, I'm sure glad you showed up," Matthew said. "I needed some help here."

"No Matt, you're doing fine. He's right Corey, give the sermon tomorrow. Worship and prayer have to go on, through births and deaths."

Deaths. Both his fathers. Corey broke down, falling against Matthew's shoulder. Matthew held him. "I know man," he said. "I know."

Jay stood next to them. When Corey's sobbing faded, Jay decided to add some light warmth to the mix. "Say Corey, what did you think about your roommate at Monterey Bible College?"

Corey sniffed. "My roommate? You mean Chuck?"

"Do you remember his last name?"

"Los Ang...no, *de* Angeles."

"Now, what does that mean?"

"I don't know."

"Sure you do. Where's your high school Spanish?"

Corey thought, his head still on Matthew's

GARY KYRIAZI

shoulder. "From the angels, *of* the angels." He looked up at Jay. "Do you mean...."

"I liked the Bob Dylan tee shirt," Jay grinned. "I thought it was a nice touch."

Corey pulled back from Matthew and wiped his eyes with his sleeve.

"Atta boy," Jay said. "Now," he put his hands on Matthew and Corey's backs and guided them to the front door., "Corey, you go see to your mother, Matthew go see to your wife. In a little while I'll tell Ralph that he'll also speak tomorrow at church. He'll tell everyone what Sal did." He opened the door and ushered them inside.

"Hey!" Corey turned around when the door shut behind them. It was just he and Matthew inside the door. He opened the door and looked out. The deck was empty.

"Yeah," Matthew quipped, "He does that."

TWENTY

Takin' it to the streets!

Takin' it to the streets!

Sal didn't hit the rocks as he expected, but landed softly on his feet on the shoulder of Highway 1, across from his church. He heard the Doobie Brothers song, increasing in volume, coming from the south, heading into town.

Takin' it to the streets!

Takin' it to the streets!

The red, four-wheel-drive Ford F-250 pulled over next to Sal. The automatic passenger window went down.

"Jay!" Sal exclaimed.

"Hop in Sal."

Sal opened the door and climbed in. "Where's Barney?"

"He's asleep in the back. He had quite a workout today."

"I'll bet he did." Sal looked around for the seat belt.

"There aren't any," Jay told him, ejecting the cassette from the tape deck.

"Hey, keep playing that," Sal said, "I always liked that song."

"Well Bud, you're past it now. You already took it to the streets, and you did a pretty decent job of it too, better than you ever gave yourself credit for."

Sal gave a humble grin.

"But Sal, if you'll forgive an observation, you and your buddy Pete sure like to go out with a bang, like you were Butch Cassidy and the Sundance Kid."

"Yeah well..." Sal shrugged. "Hey, this is Pete's truck."

"Yeah, he lets me borrow it. But I want to tell you just one thing before we hit the road."

"What's that?"

"You don't have to worry about your wife and two sons, they'll be fine. Now Connie, well that little Irish lady is a lot tougher than she knows; she'll muscle up for her new life. And your son Corey, did you see him holding his little brother?"

Sal nodded. "I caught a glimpse of it as I was headed down to the rocks."

"Corey has just found purpose in his young life. He'll raise his little brother. He and Freeman will grow up together."

All Sal could do was smile, even laugh. He

never knew such joy was possible. Never on Earth.

"Okay Sal, ready to head north?"

Sal nodded.

Jay put the truck into first, checked his mirrors, and let the clutch out. Once in fourth gear and the road was theirs, he grabbed another cassette from the dashboard and pushed it into the tape deck.

America's "Ventura Highway" began to play.

CPSIA information can be obtained
at www.ICGtesting.com
Printed in the USA
LVHW080002120421
683999LV00052B/68/J

9 781977 238917